VIRGIN TERRITORY

Mary Piper was wearing a long, blue velvet robe when she opened her hotel room door. The robe was parted slightly in front and Bolt saw that she wore nothing under it. As he stepped into the room he avoided looking down at her thighs where the robe was parted even more.

Mary closed the door, then turned and faced him.

"I've been thinking about you after you left this afternoon," she said. "Most men would have taken advantage of me. But I admire you for treating me like a lady."

Before Bolt could speak she stood on tiptoes, wrapped her arms around his neck, and put her lips on his. Then she broke the kiss and took a deep breath.

"Bolt?" she asked huskily.

"Yeah?" he answered.

"What's it like being a harlot?"

BOLT

An Adult Western Series by Cort Martin

Available wherever paperbacks are sold, or order direct from the Publisher. Send cover price plus 50¢ per copy for mailing and handling to Zebra Books, Dept. 1866, 475 Park Avenue South, New York, N.Y. 10016. DO NOT SEND CASH.

BOLT #20

SIX-GUNS AND SILK

BY
CORT MARTIN

ZEBRA BOOKS
KENSINGTON PUBLISHING CORP.

ZEBRA BOOKS

are published by

Kensington Publishing Corp.
475 Park Avenue South
New York, NY 10016

First printing: July 1986

Printed in the United States of America

Chapter One

Jack Ramsey stood motionless in the obscure shadows of the cottonwood trees. He didn't want to be seen.

Ramsey, a tall, heartless outlaw, focused his binoculars on the Indian girl in the meadow below him. He sucked in a quick breath and studied the girl's budding curves as she bent down to dip her bucket in the stream. A pretty young thing, she was. Soft and pliable, yet tight and firm. A sensual Indian maiden who couldn't be more than sixteen or seventeen, he figured. Just ripe for the plucking.

Heading for Cow Town near San Antonio, Ramsey and his small band of desperados had ridden hard all morning across the dry, dusty Texas trails. When they'd stopped to rest a few minutes before, it had been the sound of a gurgling stream that had caught Ramsey's attention and caused him to walk over to the row of trees beyond the road, where he discovered that there was a small meadow below him that had been cut away and smoothed over by the eroding flood waters of the river many years before.

The quiet meadow, its tall grasses dotted by clumps of blue lupine, seemed so out of place there on the rugged prairie of southern Texas. It had surprised him to see the river down there when he thought that the closest river was way south and west of them. He'd thought all along that they'd been riding across flat, open land that was only occasionally broken up by clumps of trees. It had startled him even more to gaze down into the valley and see the girl down there.

Now, as he peered through the binoculars, the pretty, young Indian maiden seemed like a mirage that had magically materialized out of the oppressive heat of the August day. A sexual fantasy brought to life.

Ramsey, the violent, vindictive leader of the small gang of ruthless bandits, stood perfectly still on the bluff, tucked amid the thick cottonwoods and sturdy oaks, so that he couldn't be seen by anyone who might look up his way from the small Indian camp that was nestled in the wide, flat valley.

Filled with a sudden lust, he licked his lips and gloated over his discovery. He flexed his muscles, felt their power. A smile warped his thin lips as he considered a slight change in his plans to extract his revenge from the man named Bolt.

Thin blades of grass bent under his dusty boots and then were trampled flat when the big, broad-shouldered outlaw lowered the binoculars and turned around. With that slight movement, the stench of his sweat-drenched shirt drifted up to his nostrils. He breathed the smell in deeply and felt very manly. A limb creaked as he pushed it aside so that he could see his friends beyond the thick foliage.

For a long minute, he watched the six rough, tough fellows who made up his outlaw band. Three of the men puffed on hand-rolled cigarettes while they waited for him near the restless horses back there on the road. Two others, Kyle Hutchinson and Oppie Shenker, sucked on their whiskey flasks.

The youngest member of the group was eighteen-year-old, blond-headed Vernon Tate, who got his dander up if anybody called him a kid. Tate's head jerked from side to side as he suspiciously eyed his surroundings, his pale blue eyes restless agates in their sockets. He constantly scanned the countryside with wide eyes, and because his mouth usually hung open Tate always looked like he was half crazy. Whenever Ramsey looked at the boy, he expected to see spittle drooling down from the corners of Tate's slack mouth. But it hadn't taken Ramsey long to realize that the kid was a whole lot smarter than most of the folks Ramsey knew. Besides that, Tate's eccentric alertness to his surroundings had paid off for Ramsey's band of thieves more than once when they were pulling off a robbery.

His men were a grubby-looking bunch, Ramsey thought, as he looked at their old grimy blue jeans, faded shirts, and battered hats. Even Fester Grodin, a former crooked politician who considered himself a ladies' man, looked slovenly. Fester always wore a leather vest over a white shirt in an attempt to show everybody that he had class, but his shirt was frayed, badly stained, and Fester looked just as shabby as the rest of them.

Ramsey didn't care. Appearances didn't matter much to him. Action and loyalty did. Every member of his outlaw band was fearless, mean as hell and completely loyal to him. That's what counted with Ramsey. All six of his men happened to be damned good at their chosen craft, too, which was why Ramsey had picked them to work with him.

Robbing banks was their specialty, but they were just as talented at raiding a train or holding up a stagecoach when they knew there'd be a substantial amount of gold or cash on board. They didn't mess with small change, but made it their business to find out which banks would have a big hunk of cash on hand or which train or stage carried a worthwhile sum of payroll money to one of the isolated forts. The gang members also made it their business to outwit the members of rival outlaw bands who might have the same idea, the same information.

Ramsey prided himself on his gang's record and took full credit for their accomplishments. During the two years they'd been together, Ramsey's outlaws had pulled off more than fifty profitable holdups. A pretty good score, he thought. And not a single one of his boys had ever been caught by the law, even though they'd killed a few innocent men in their greedy pursuit of the money.

He was glad now that they'd stopped at that particular spot on the road to stretch their legs. If he hadn't strolled over to the clump of trees and looked down into the valley where he'd heard the rushing waters of the river, he wouldn't have spotted the Indian camp in the valley below. And if he hadn't seen the Indian girl, he wouldn't have come up with the idea of dragging the Indians into his little scheme for revenge against Bolt.

He smiled, took in a deep breath, let his chest swell with pride as he mulled over the ingenious plan that was forming in his mind. He considered himself smarter than anyone else when it came to scheming and he was always impressed by his own intelligence.

He knew his men wouldn't mind a change of plans. They were eager to help him settle the score with the man named Bolt. They didn't like what Bolt had done to Ramsey's poor little sister any better than Ramsey did. And even if they had qualms about carrying out his new plans, the outlaws wouldn't balk. Ramsey was the boss and they did what he said. Without question. They were mean sons of bitches, but they were staunchly loyal to him, and he trusted them completely.

The hot Texas breeze flapped at his loose shirt and

cooled his sweaty skin, but did nothing to take away Ramsey's terrible hangover thirst. Since he didn't want to walk back to his horse for his canteen just then, he fished a shaggy twist of tobacco out of his pocket, ripped a big chunk of the tobacco off with brown-stained teeth, and began chewing it to soften it up. He stuffed the twist back in his pocket, turned around to face the Indian camp again, and brought the binoculars back up to his eyes.

The fabric of his pants leg bunched up in small wrinkles where the thongs of his holster were tied low around his thigh. He carried a Remington .44, converted pistol in the holster and had a pearl-handled hideout Deringer .41 tucked into his waistband.

Standing with his feet apart to balance himself, he focused the binoculars on the river that bubbled across rocks and boulders as it picked its way through the contour of the valley. He swung the binoculars around until he found the pretty Indian girl again, then moved his head slowly, following her movement. His loins flashed with heat when he saw the young maiden's buttocks bounce beneath her tight buckskin dress as she struggled with the heavy bucket of water that she carried from the stream.

With the weight of the water pulling her right shoulder down, the young Indian maiden shuffled along a dirt path. Her long, dark braids skipped across her shoulders, bounced against the back of her dress as she made her way back to the small camp. Even with her short, careful steps, the water sloshed over the rim of the full pail and spilled down her smooth, bare legs and splattered across her dusty moccasins.

Ramsey pulled the binoculars away from his eyes just long enough to spit a stream of tobacco juice to the ground. He brushed the brown spittle from the stubble of beard on his chin, then wiped his hand across his

9

already-stained trousers. He jammed the glasses up to his eyes again, leered at the bronze-skinned girl as she set the bucket down on the dry ground where three other Indian women were gathered around the fire ring. The women spoke to each other, but Ramsey couldn't hear their voices above the gurgling of the stream.

He noticed that the inside rocks of the fire ring were scorched but not totally blackened. This was a temporary camp for the small Indian tribe and Ramsey wondered why there were no Indian men around.

The muscular outlaw leader shifted his focus to another girl, the one who kneeled on the ground in front of a low, flat rock. The girl's fingers worked a clump of dough in a big clay bowl that rested in her lap. She was turned sideways, which gave Ramsey a good view of her firm breasts that swelled beneath her buckskin dress, her thin waistline, and her nicely-rounded buttocks that stretched the material taut. His crotch burned hot when he saw that this girl, like the maiden who had carried the water, was young, pretty, and as desirable as they came.

He moved his head only slightly, glanced at the other two women, lost interest in them when he saw that they were matronly, thick-waisted, full-faced squaws who wore shapeless buckskin garments and rows of colorful beads around their plump necks.

Ramsey scanned the small camp, the grassy area around it. They were Comanches. He knew that by the markings on the double row of teepees which were arranged in a half-circle beyond the fire ring. Five teepees in the inside row, six more behind those. Smoke curled from the top of the middle lodge, which obviously belonged to the chief. The drawings on this teepee were more elaborate than on the others and near the door flap hung a long plume of brightly colored feathers, and next to the feathers was something that looked like a string of scalplocks.

He saw no Indian men at all, no small children. Except for the four Indian ponies that grazed at the ends of long tethers, there were no other horses in sight. He figured that the Indian braves were gone from this temporary camp to hunt food for the small tribe. Or maybe they were on the warpath. Either way, Jack Ramsey hoped that the braves wouldn't return until evening. It was nearly two in the afternoon and he needed time to carry out his plans.

He swung the binoculars back to the four women and watched one of the plump squaws dip a small clay bowl into the bucket. The woman let the bowl fill with water, then carried it to the middle teepee where she disappeared inside. The other matronly squaw ladled water into a big pot, set the pot over the fire, then strolled over to another teepee where she went inside and pulled the flap closed behind her. Ramsey's gaze went back to the two young maidens.

"How long are you gonna stare down at them injuns?" Kyle Hutchinson asked as he limped up behind Ramsey and glanced down at the valley below. Hutch, as his outlaw friends called him, was as thin as a scrub pine. His shoulders hunched forward, and the way his back curved like a question mark, he looked like he had no chest at all. Even so, the muscles that didn't show were all powerful.

Hutch was, by far, the most treacherous of the seven-member outlaw band. He had no regard for life, no fear of death, because he saw himself as mystically immortal. Instead of hating the ugly purple scar that ran down the left side of his face and across his throat, and the old twin bullet wounds that left him with a bad limp and a lot of pain, he was proud of these disfigurements because they served as his proof to the world that he couldn't be killed.

"Jist long enough to make sure there ain't no injun braves around," Ramsey said.

"I thought you was in a hurry to get to Bolt's ranch," Hutch sighed. In a gesture of boredom, he reached up and broke a dead twig from the tree, snapped it in half and tossed it to the ground.

"Not that much of a hurry." Ramsey took the binoculars away from his face, spit the entire wad of tobacco out. "Besides, I think I've just found a way to get Bolt so deep in trouble, the bastard'll drown in his own stinkin' asshole."

"You're talkin' in circles, Ram."

"Look for yourself. Comanches." Ramsey handed the binoculars to Hutch. The thin outlaw took them, peered through the twin lenses.

"So? I don't see nothin' but two injun gals down there." Kyle Hutchinson looked up at his boss, shrugged his rounded shoulders. "How in the hell are they gonna help you get rid of Bolt?"

"Ha. I've got it all figured out up here," Ramsey snorted, tapping the side of his head. "Comanches are good trackers, ain't they?"

"Yeah, good trackers and damned good horsemen, too, but they're mean as the devil himself. I wouldn't mess with 'em if I didn't have to, Ram. I think it'd be best if we just rode on."

"You ain't scared of 'em, are ya, Hutch?" Ramsey taunted.

"Hell, no. I ain't a-scaired of nobody. You know that. Besides, there ain't been nobody born yet who's smart enough to track us down," Hutch boasted. When he grinned, the scar on his cheek puckered and pulled the corner of his lip up at a crooked angle that showed the gaps inside his mouth where teeth were missing. He handed the binoculars back to Ramsey.

"You're right about that, Hutch. That's why we're gonna make it easy for them dumb injuns to follow us."

Hutch shook his head. "Why in hell would you want them savage Comanches to follow us? You been hittin' the bottle a little hard this morning?"

"I got my reasons," Ramsey said, a cold determination to his voice.

"And what in the hell makes you think they'd want to track us anyway?" Puzzled, Hutch snapped another dead twig from the tree, broke it in half with an easy flick of the wrists, then tossed it to the ground.

"Let me put it this way. If you was a Comanche brave and somebody stole your purty Indian maidens, you'd damned sure smear the war paint on, wouldn't you?" Ramsey said, his brown eyes dark and narrowed to slits, a smug smile playing at his lips.

"Damned right I would. But what I don't understand is why the hell you want them Comanche bastards tracking our asses."

"Not ours. Bolt's. And those two pretty little Indians maidens are gonna be our bait."

Chapter Two

Ramsey glanced over his shoulder when he heard the movement behind him, the crunch of footsteps.

"What purty Indian maidens?" Fess Grodin beamed as he strolled up behind Ramsey. "Are we missing something?" Fess stood up tall, straightened his old leather vest. He slipped his hat off, smoothed his dark brown hair into place with dirty fingers, then slid the battered hat back in place.

"Whatcha all lookin' at?" Big Mac Sloan called out in his booming voice as he walked up and stood near the others. Sloan shrugged his wide shoulders as he peered down into the valley. He was a giant of a man, tall, with a full barrel chest that sloped down to his huge belly and the roll of fat that hung over the top of his pants. Although he was almost bald and always wore a hat to cover his bare head, he grew a full, bushy beard and a thick moustache.

"Not so loud, dammit," Ramsey cautioned the men in a hushed voice. "Down there." He gestured toward the valley with a nod of his head, then handed the binoculars to Fess Grodin.

"Ha, you know who they are?" Fess exclaimed after he'd peered through the double lenses.

"Comanches," Ramsey said, a whiskey husk to his

voice.

"Yeah. That's Yellow Dog's tribe. In fact, that's Chief Yellow Dog's daughter, Little Killdeer. The one kneeling down with a bowl in her lap." Fess lowered the binoculars, glanced over at Ramsey. "You remember them injuns Sloan and I ran into about a month back? The ones we traded that rotgut whiskey to in exchange for some of their deer meat?"

"I remember," Ramsey frowned. "They donned their war bonnets and took out after the whole damned bunch of us when they discovered that you'd watered down that whiskey."

"But they didn't catch us," Fess bragged. "Didn't even come close."

"The chief's daughter, hmmm," Ramsey mused. "That could be a big help to us."

"Let me see," Big Mac Sloan insisted, reaching out for the binoculars. He nudged the others aside with his fat belly as he moved into the tight cluster of men.

"Here, see for yourself," Fess said as he handed the field glasses over.

"Sure enough, that's those same injuns," Big Mac smiled. "And there's Plover Egg, standin' there, purty as a picture. She's Gray Wolf's sister."

"Who the hell is Gray Wolf?" Hutch asked. He snapped another twig in half and tossed it aside.

"He's one dangerous injun with a damned short fuse," Sloan said in a deep voice that came from somewhere within his huge chest. "He's the real leader of the tribe, far as I could tell."

"I think you're right about Gray Wolf being the real power," Fester Grodin agreed. "That night we tangled with 'em, old Chief Yellow Dog looked too poorly to be anything but a respected figurehead."

"That makes things even better," Ramsey commented, thinking out loud.

Big Mac Sloan ignored Ramsey's remarks and glanced through the binoculars again. "Ah, yes," he sighed, "if Gray Wolf hadn't been such a mean, arrogant son of a bitch, I'd have taken Plover Egg into the bushes that night. I sure wanted to dip my wick into that tight little pussy of hers. Still do," he laughed crudely.

"Just give me Little Killdeer and I'd be happier than a pig in shit," Fess said.

"Don't worry, fellows," Ramsey smiled smugly. "You'll get your way with those two Indian wenches soon enough. In fact, we'll all have our way with them."

"Let's get to it," Fess Grodin panted.

Ramsey took the binoculars back from Sloan and had one more look at the Indian maidens. He swung the glasses slowly and scanned the camp again to make sure there were no men around. He studied the terrain, spotted a place off to his left where he could ride down the hillside to the camp. Satisfied, he lowered the binoculars.

"Oh, yes," Ramsey beamed, "this is gonna be as easy as shootin' the ass off a chicken with a blunderbuss at five feet." He stroked his stubbled chin. "And knowing that them gals are important to the tribe makes my plans even more brilliant."

"What plans?" Fester Grodin asked, a puzzled expression on his face. "I thought we were going to Bolt's whorehouse to knock his lights out."

"We are, but I've come up with a new plan and those injun virgins are gonna help our cause. Someday you'll all realize just how smart I am." After one more glance down the hill, Ramsey whirled around, headed for the road. Short mesquite bushes bent and broke as the three outlaws followed their determined leader.

"Saddle up, men," Ramsey ordered when he reached his own dust-flecked horse. He took a long drink of water from his canteen, then hung the canteen strap back over the saddlehorn. The stiff leather creaked as he mounted his stallion and settled into the new saddle that had been purchased with money stolen during the gang's last bank holdup. He leaned over, adjusted the Winchester .44 rifle that hung in a scabbard on the right side of his horse, then drew himself up tall and watched the others move toward their mounts.

"Tate, you and Wiley ride on up ahead with Big Mac," he commanded. "Wait for us about a mile up the road. And keep your eyes and ears open."

"Oh, we will. Don't you worry about a thing," said Vernon Tate who was constantly eyeing his surroundings anyway.

"Fess, you and Shenker ride back down the trail a ways and have a look-see. Then ride on up and join the others," Ramsey said. "I don't want no surprises."

"What in the hell are we lookin' for?" Oppie Shenker asked in his slow, southern drawl. He took another swig of whiskey from his flask and stuffed it in his saddlebag before he mounted his horse.

"Anything that moves," Ramsey snapped. "Especially if it's got red skin. Hutch, you come on with me. We'll get the girls. Then we'll go take care of Bolt."

Dust kicked up from the parched earth and clouded the air as the outlaws' horses dug their hooves into the hard ground and took off in different directions. After the others were gone, Kyle Hutchinson jerked his reins to his left, guided his horse over next to Jack Ramsey.

Ramsey sat tall in the saddle, watching his men ride away. His head was turned away from Hutch.

"Think you're makin' a big mistake, Ram," Hutch suggested.

"Oh? How so?" Ramsey chuckled without turning to face Hutch.

"Kidnapping those Indian girls is serious business

17

and I don't really think it'll work to our advantage." Unlike the others in the gang, Hutchinson wasn't afraid to speak up to Ramsey.

Ramsey swung around in the saddle. His eyes darkened as he studied his friend's face. "It'll work, dammit. When we get through with those two girls, the injuns are gonna think that Bolt and that swine partner of his, Tom Penrod, were the ones who kidnapped and raped their precious maidens. I'll see to that. I'm gonna make damned sure that Bolt gets what he deserves. The bastard!"

"You really hate Bolt, don't you?" Hutch said, giving the outlaw leader a sideways glance.

"I hate that son of a bitch more than anyone I've ever known." Ramsey leaned over the side of his horse and spit to the ground to show his contempt, to vent his seething rage.

"But you don't even know Bolt," Hutch reasoned. "You've never even seen him."

"I know who he is and that's enough for me. That bastard turned my sister into a whore."

"Seems to me you're lettin' this thing about your sister eat your guts away. It's mucking up your brain, Ram."

"You sayin' I'm crazy?" Ramsey's head snapped around and he glared at his friend.

"Hell, no, but ever since that night we went to Bolt's whorehouse and you spotted your sister working there, that's all you've talked about."

"That's all I've thought about, dammit," Ramsey said through clenched teeth. Every muscle in his body tightened up on him again. Without realizing he was doing it, his hands doubled up to hard fists as the hatred boiled up inside him. His eyes narrowed to thin slits.

"If you were so riled up about Linda workin' there,

why didn't you find Bolt that night and pound the piss out of him, or even kill him? Or why didn't you just jerk Linda out of there, right then and there? Then it would've been over and done with right quick. But now, the way this rage is building up inside you, you're about to burst wide open with it."

"Because I didn't want Linda to see me there," Ramsey said in a cold, even voice. "That's why I didn't do something about it that night. I didn't want her to know that I'd found out about her evil ways. I'm sure it would have been embarrassing to both of us."

"Maybe your sister's a whore because she wants to be," Hutch suggested. "Did you ever think of that, Ram?"

"Not my little Linda," Ramsey roared. "You know damned well I raised her right." He felt his cheeks flush with anger.

"I know you did the very best you could with her under the tragic circumstances," Hutch said, trying to calm his friend.

"Look, Linda was only ten years old when our folks died and it was my responsibility to take care of her after that. And I did it, dammit!"

"And you resented every damned minute of it."

"Maybe some, but I took care of her without belly-achin' about it. I could've sent her off to an orphanage where they didn't care beans about her, or I could've dumped her with some stupid neighbors. But I didn't." Ramsey felt beads of perspiration pop out on his forehead. He took a deep breath, and then another. "I took care of Linda for eight long years, until she was old enough to be on her own." He clenched his fists again and felt the old resentments building up inside. "Dammit, I gave up my freedom for her. I stayed home with her all the time instead of going out carousing like all the other fellows did. And this is the damned thanks

I get. Hell, I didn't even get a chance to court any of the pretty young ladies when I wanted to, just because of my sister."

"You can't blame Linda for that," Hutch said in a low, calm voice.

"I wanted to set a good example for her. And, believe me, I taught Linda to be a good girl. When she finally left home, I thought she was going off to college like a nice little girl. I thought I'd be proud of her. But where does she end up? Spreading her legs for any man with a dollar in his pocket," Ramsey raged.

"Calm down, Jack."

"A goddamned harlot in Bolt's filthy damned whorehouse. That's what she is. And it's all Bolt's fault. He turned my sister into a whore. He's just using her to make money for himself, the greedy goddamned bastard. Now Linda's a ruined woman."

"You haven't exactly been a saint, Ram. Being an outlaw . . ."

"She never knew about any of that. Besides, that's got nothing to do with Linda," Jack snapped, his face flushed with anger. He looked away from his friend, stared down at his saddlehorn, tried to control his temper. "Dammit! I raised Linda to be a good, decent girl, and I hate Bolt with all my heart for making her a whore."

"You know, Ram," Hutch said in a gentle voice, "my grandpappy used to tell me to be careful of what you hate in other people, because most of the time, it's the very same thing you hate about yourself."

Ramsey's head jerked up. He frowned at his friend.

"What's that supposed to mean?" he demanded. He whipped a red bandanna from his pocket and wiped the sweat from his forehead.

"Just tryin' to be helpful. Forget it."

But Ramsey wouldn't let it go. "Are you insinuating

that it's all my fault that I hate Bolt so damned much?" he ranted. "Hell, you'd be mad too, if it'd been your sister that Bolt had turned into a two-bit whore."

"I ain't insinuating anything, Ram. I just want you to think about it. Think about your anger, your blind hatred—where it's coming from. It ain't doing you any good, that's for damned sure."

"I didn't turn Linda into a whore!" Ramsey raged. "That bastard Bolt did it!"

A fierce anger raced through Jack Ramsey's veins and rushed to the surface, like the fiery lava of an erupting volcano. He fought back the flood of hatred that threatened to explode his brain. He knew damned well that his uncontrollable wrath was directed only at Bolt. He wanted the bastard to suffer for what he'd done.

But there was something else, too. Something more than his vehement hatred for the man named Bolt. The sudden, intense feelings of violence that raged inside him just then, he realized, had been brought on, or at least heightened, by what his friend had just said.

He glared at Hutch, briefly hating him, too, because Hutch knew.

Kyle Hutchinson's simple words about hatred had touched something buried so deep in Ramsey's mind and heart that he hadn't even known it was there.

But now, those feelings of guilt that he had buried for so long, those thoughts that he wouldn't ever allow himself to think, had all surfaced full bloom.

And for the first time, Ramsey had to face those uncomfortable feelings, those ugly thoughts that made him squirm.

Jack Ramsey had to wonder if he himself had been the one responsible for his own sister becoming a whore.

Chapter Three

The stagecoach from Fort Worth was late. It always was when the heat was so bad.

Jared Bolt shaded his eyes from the bright sun and looked up the main street of San Antonio where the stage would be coming around the corner soon. Nothing. But he knew it would be along shortly. Some fellow had just ridden in and said he'd passed the lumbering stage a ways out of town.

Bolt stepped back and leaned against the building where a slice of shade gave him some relief from the boiling sun. He reached in his pocket for the makings of a cigarette and, instead, pulled out the three-page letter he'd received the day before. The heady fragrance of the perfumed pages floated up to his nostrils and got him to wondering about her again. He unfolded the wrinkled papers and read the letter for the fifth time.

Dear Mr. Bolt,

You don't know me but my Aunt Millie, Millicent Piper, passed away a week ago this Monday evening. I wouldn't trouble you with this sad news except that Aunt Mille told me about you and said that she was a good friend of yours and I thought you would want to know of her passing. I also wanted to assure you that the illness that took her was short and she didn't suffer much.

Please don't think me presumptuous, but there is another reason why I am writing to you. Aunt Millie said that if anything happened to her, that I should contact you and that you would take care of me. She left me a little money, but not enough for me to live on without making other arrangements.

Please don't get me wrong. I wouldn't expect you to be financially responsible for me under any circumstances. Aunt Millie said that you employ a few girls there at your Rocking Bar Ranch and I would appreciate the opportunity to work for you, too.

Although I have never done exactly that kind of work, I think I am well qualified and I know that I would enhance your business. I am twenty-one years old, not beautiful, but pretty enough, as Aunt Millie used to tell me. I have limber legs, tight muscles, and an agile body. I know all of the proper movements and I can go fast or slow, depending on the needs of your customers. I can teach a man all he wants to know in an hour, if time permits me that long with one man. I might even teach you a new thing or two.

I wouldn't bother you with this request, Mr. Bolt, but I'm desperate and I don't know who else to turn to. Aunt Millie told me that you were a decent man and that you treated women with respect, so I'm sure I would be happy working for you.

I don't want to risk your turning me down without giving me a chance, so this letter is to inform you that I will arrive in San Antonio on

Friday, August 15th on the two o'clock stage. Would you be kind enough to meet the stage? I'll wear my red dress so you'll be sure to recognize me, although possibly, I may be the only woman on the stage.

I will be anxious to start work right away.

Yours truly,
Mary Beth Piper

Bolt folded the letter and flipped it against the palm of his hand, still somewhat puzzled by it. When he'd received the letter, he'd remembered Millicent Piper right away and he was truly saddened by the news of her death. But he had cursed, too. He didn't want the responsibility of taking care of Millie's niece.

Millie Piper had been the neighbor of the rancher he'd bought some cattle from up in Fort Worth and she'd been kind enough to put him up for the few days that it had taken him to complete the cattle transaction. A widow woman who said she was glad for the company, Millie had fed him and washed his clothes and played the piano for him while they sang joyously together. And because they had gotten along so well, Millie had taken him to her bed.

During the time he stayed at Millie's farmhouse, there wasn't a young girl there, but he remembered vaguely that she had mentioned that her young, orphaned niece would be coming to live with her.

The thing that puzzled Bolt was why Millie would send her niece to him when Millie had found it hard to believe that he ran a bordello on his ranch. He'd been honest about it when she'd asked him about his life, but he'd gotten the impression that she disapproved of bordellos and certainly of the type of women who worked there.

The part of Mary Beth's letter that bothered him was

that she said that she hadn't done exactly that kind of work. What did that mean? He'd never turned a woman into a whore and he wasn't about to start now. Obviously, Mary Beth knew what she was getting into, though. In fact, the part about her limber legs and tight muscles had even given Bolt a twinge in his loins. But she wouldn't get the chance to teach him a new thing or two. Bolt didn't sleep with the girls who worked for him. It was one of his hard-and-fast rules.

He wondered what she looked like. Not beautiful, but pretty enough, according to Millie. Fat. He'd bet anything Mary Beth was fat, now that he thought about it. After all, Millie had been pleasantly plump.

"You still waiting?"

Bolt turned his head and saw his tall, lanky friend, Tom Penrod, walking toward him.

"Yeah. I was just thinking about going across the street and having a drink. Want to join me?"

"No. I think I'll head on out to the ranch. I got all the supplies we needed. They're loaded in the buckboard and you can bring them out when the girl comes."

"She's fat, Tom. I just know she is."

"Who's fat?"

"Mary Beth Piper. Fat girls always use too much perfume. Here, smell this." Bolt shoved the letter under Tom's nose.

"Hmmm, smells mighty good to me. Sexy. Just remember, thin girls use perfume, too."

"Hell, Tom, you wouldn't know anything about girls except what's between their legs."

"That's what counts, isn't it?"

"You got no class, Tom. Mary Beth is gonna be wearing a red dress, too."

"What's that supposed to prove?"

"Fat girls wear red dresses when they should wear black or dark blue," Bolt grumbled. He stuffed the letter back in his pocket.

"Hell, she's gonna be one of your harlots, not a Sunday-School teacher."

"I know."

"Some men prefer a gal who's got a little meat on her bones, you know. It makes for a softer roll in the hay. So what's wrong with fat girls?"

"Nothing, Tom, I'm just talking through my hat. Waiting for the stage in this heat has got my imagination running wild. I just got to wondering what Mary Beth would look like."

"You want me to wait for this Piper gal so you can go on home?" Tom grinned. "I wouldn't mind trying her out for you. Tubby or skinny, I don't care."

"No thanks, Tom. Wouldn't want you to wear yourself out on my account."

"Suit yourself. Ah ha," Tom said as he turned around and glanced up the street, "Looks like your waiting is over."

Bolt heard the rumbling noise, too, and stretched his neck to see the stagecoach rounding the corner and coming down the street in a whirl of dust. A few minutes later, the stage came to an abrupt stop in front of the stage-stop office where Bolt and Tom were waiting. The coach rocked back and forth, creaked on its hinges, then finally settled down as the dust began to clear.

Bolt hung back, stayed on the boardwalk near the building. He felt a nervous twinge in the pit of his stomach as he watched the driver jump down from the driver's seat and walk around to open the stage door. His heart skipped a beat when he saw the flash of red dress as the first passenger appeared in the doorway. His heart sank as the woman took the driver's hand and emerged from the coach. The woman looked around at her surroundings, smiled at Bolt when she

26

saw him looking at her.

"Looks like you were right, Bolt. Did you see that stagecoach rise up two feet when she got off? And I do believe I can smell her perfume from here," Tom grinned. He elbowed Bolt playfully and sniffed the air. "Good thing you brought the Springfield wagon to town today. You'd be in fine fettle if you had to ride double on Nick with that ball of blubber."

"Shut up, Tom," Bolt said out of the corner of his mouth. "Like you said, some men prefer them a little plump."

"You call that plump?" Tom chuckled. "See you back at the ranch, if the horse can still pull the weight of the buckboard. Should have brought the whole team."

"May the big black buzzards shit on your saddle," Bolt said dryly.

"And may your wagon wheels not break when you load your new cow." Tom tipped his hat and walked away, grinning.

Bolt watched his friend stroll down the street to the hitchrail where Tom's horse was tied up next to the horse that pulled Bolt's Springfield wagon. Tom paused at the buckboard, pushed down on the flat bed a couple of times as if to test its springs. He looked back at Bolt and shrugged his shoulders before he mounted his horse and rode away. Bolt shook his head, then turned his attention to the stagecoach.

A nicely-dressed man stepped down from the stage-coach next. He turned around and offered his hand up to another female passenger, who also happened to be wearing a red dress. The difference was, the second woman to get off the coach wore a dress that clung to her slender, sensual figure. Two other passengers, both men, followed her out of the coach.

For a minute, Bolt got his hopes up. Until he saw the fat woman make her way across the boardwalk and waddle toward him with a big smile on her face. He swallowed hard, took a step toward the woman.

"Are you Miss Piper?" he asked politely as he took off his Stetson.

"Oh, no," she said. "I'm Elizabeth Snyder. A Mr. Thomas Davis sent for me to be his bride. I was hoping you were Mr. Davis."

"Sorry." Bolt sighed and hoped it didn't show. "I saw Tommy go into the saloon across the street a little while ago. I'm sure he'll be back over here soon."

"That's Mary Beth over by the stagecoach," Miss Snyder said, nodding toward the pretty girl in red. "She's a lucky lady to have someone like you here to meet her. I just hope Mr. Davis is half as handsome as you are."

"He's a good man and not bad-looking," Holt assured her. "Good luck, Miss Snyder."

"Thanks. You too."

Bolt felt like he was walking on air as he strolled over to the stage, Stetson in hand.

"Pardon me, are you Miss Piper?" he said, smelling the familiar perfume.

"Yes. Are you Mr. Bolt?"

"Yes, ma'am."

A smile broke across the girl's face and Bolt melted. Mary Beth had that same sparkle in her deep blue eyes that her Aunt Millie had had. The same sensual smile that had caused Bolt's heart to flutter. The same dimples in her cheeks, and Bolt was a sucker for dimples. But the resemblance ended there.

Mary Beth was actually pretty while Millie had been attractive, but plain-looking. Millie had long, dark hair, tied back in a bun. Mary Beth's hair was blonde and the way the sun fell on it, the fine strands looked as if they had been spun from honey. Except for the small wisps of hair that the breeze tossed against her cheeks, and the wavy bangs that covered her forehead, she wore her hair in soft, bouncy curls that were pulled back away from her face and secured at the back of her head. The curls seemed to cascade down from the small, red, feathered hat that perched on top of her head.

Bolt knew he was staring at Mary Beth too long, but he didn't seem to be able to take his eyes off her.

"Uh, sorry to hear about Millie," he said, finally.

"Me too. Her death was a shock, coming so soon after my pa passed away."

"What about your mother?" Bolt asked, shifting his gaze to the stagecoach driver who was on top of the coach, lowering the baggage to the three gentlemen passengers who took it from him and set it on the boardwalk.

"She died when I was twelve. Oh, here, this is my bag," she said, reaching for the suitcase that had just been placed on the wooden planks.

"Let me." Bolt picked up the heavy carpetbag. "Are you hungry?"

"Not really. But I'm thirsty."

"Let's get something to drink before we head out to the ranch."

After a few steps, Mary Beth stumbled, bumped against Bolt, then hooked her arm through his.

"Guess I don't have my land legs back yet."

"I won't let you fall." They smiled at each other and Bolt wanted to draw her closer, put his arm around her. Even so, he felt her heat, her softness.

He stopped at the buckboard long enough to put her carpetbag on the wagon bed and tie it down. Then he took her to the nearby cafe where he ordered sarsaparilla for both of them.

"You loved my Aunt Millie, didn't you?" Mary Beth asked as she sipped her drink.

29

"I only knew her for a very short time, but I was very fond of her. She was quite a lady."

"I guess she had a mind to marry you, but she said you weren't the marrying kind."

"I reckon not," Bolt smiled. "Not yet, anyway. Someday I'd like to settle down and have a family of my own, I think."

"Well, I can see why Aunt Millie fell in love with you. You're quite charming, you know."

"No, I didn't know that," Bolt grinned awkwardly. He felt a flash of heat crawl up his neck and flush his cheeks, and wondered if it showed. He studied her face, her mannerisms, the open honesty in her expressions, and realized how much like her Aunt Millie she was. Mary Beth had such an innocent look about her, Bolt found it hard to picture her as a harlot. Maybe that was because he didn't want to think about her sleeping with other men. Despite the fact that he didn't want to be affected by the girl, he found himself smitten with her.

"What about the job, Mr. Bolt?" she asked suddenly. "Are you going to hire me?"

"I don't know yet, Miss Piper."

"Call me Mary," she said.

"Then call me Bolt."

"What's the matter? Am I not good enough for you?" she teased.

"Maybe you're too good."

"What do you mean by that?"

"Nothing, really. Are you sure you want the job, Mary?"

"Yes, I want the job. That's why I came all the way down here. As I told you in my letter, I'm really desperate. I inherited a little money from my father's estate, and Aunt Millie left me her house and enough money to live on for a year or two if I'm real careful.

30

But what then? . . . What do I do when the money's gone?"

"A pretty girl like you? Why you'll probably be married to some nice young fellow before long."

"I hardly think so. I don't even know any nice young fellows. Well, I do. I've danced with a few who seemed nice enough. That was after I moved in with Aunt Millie and she took me to the socials. But before that, well, my pa was very strict."

"Even so, pretty as you are, I'll bet you've had plenty of beaus fightin' for your attention."

"I wish some fellow would have come courting me," she sighed. "I've always wondered what it would be like to have a man love me. But with Papa, courting was out of the question, and with Aunt Millie it might have been different, but . . . she's gone now."

"Mary, can I ask you a personal question?"

"What's that?"

Bolt leaned across the table and spoke in a low voice, even though there were no other customers in the small cafe. "Are you a virgin?"

Mary jerked back, sat up tall, squared her shoulders, and glared at Bolt, her eyes flashing with anger.

"How dare you ask me such a rude question? I can't believe it!"

"Mary Beth, listen . . ."

"And Aunt Millie said you treated women with respect. Ha! You really had her fooled."

"No disrespect intended, miss," he tried to explain in his gentle voice, "but it's something I've got to ask before I hire you."

"You mean it actually makes a difference?" she asked her voice full of sarcasm.

"In a way it does."

"Not that it's any of your business, but, yes, of course I'm a virgin," she snapped.

31

"I figured as much." Bolt shook his head.

"Is that good or bad . . . being a virgin?" she asked, a puzzled look on her face. "You seem disappointed. I thought men preferred virgins."

"I don't hire virgins."

"Oh? I don't see what difference that makes."

"Just one of my rules."

"Mr. Bolt, I don't think you have any intention of hiring me," she accused. "I think you're just trying to make me miserable so I'll go away and leave you alone. Then you won't have to feel responsible for me just because Aunt Millie said you'd take care of me. Well, I don't give up that easy."

"It's not that I don't want you to work for me, Mary. It's just that I don't think you know what you're getting yourself into. I don't think you realize what kind of work you'd be doing."

"Yes, I do," she protested. "Aunt Millie told me that the girls who work for you entertain men who are lonely. Dance-hall girls, she said. And although I've never actually been a dance-hall girl, I know how to dance and I'd be good at it."

"I'm sure you're a good dancer." Bolt had to smile. Millie never had believed him when he'd told her that he ran a whorehouse.

"Yes, I am. I've been dancing since I was seven years old and I can do any dance there is," she pleaded. "My mother was on the stage for many years and she taught me everything she knew. It comes natural to me and I thought I could teach some of the men to dance. I just know it would improve your business. But, I explained all of this in my letter."

Bolt reached across the table and touched her hand.

"Mary, there's been a misunderanding. I run a bordello and the girls who work for me are . . . harlots. They do more than dance with the customers."

"I know what they do."

"And obviously, that's not what you had in mind when you asked for the job."

"No, it isn't." She took a sip of her drink, then lowered her head.

"I'm sorry, Mary." Bolt squeezed her hand before he withdrew his own.

Suddenly, Mary Beth looked up and stared at him with her bright blue eyes, as if she were searching for something, or trying to figure him out. Uncomfortable, Bolt shifted positions in the hard chair, but never looked away from her steady gaze.

"If that's what the job calls for, I'll do it," she announced. "After all, I don't plan to be a virgin all my life and I do like men."

"Most harlots don't like men."

"Really? Then why do they sleep with them?"

"For some it's revenge, I guess. They want to get back at every man in the world because some fellow hurt them once."

"Well, I'd do it because I like men and because I know I'd like sex. I've never made love to a man, but I came close once and I liked the tingly feeling that I got all over."

"Look, I don't hire virgins, because I think a girl's first sexual experience with a man should be something very special. It should be tender and joyful and it should happen because of a mutual love and respect the couple have for each other."

Mary Beth smiled at him. "You know, Aunt Millie was right about you. You are a decent sort, Mr. Bolt. And I still want to work for you."

"You need some time to think about this and I know you're tired from the long trip," Bolt said as he stood up and walked around the table to pull her chair out for her. "I have to go back out to the ranch, so I'm going to put you up in a hotel room for the night. I'll come back in the morning and we can talk about it then."

Bolt was relieved that Mary Beth didn't object. He escorted her to the new River Front Hotel, stopping at the buckboard on the way to get her carpetbag. She offered to pay for her room, but he insisted.

"I think you'll be comfortable here," he said as he set her bag down in the middle of the neat room, which smelled new and fresh. The curtains at the open window fluttered on the afternoon breeze and the room was pleasantly cool. A braided rug covered most of the hardwood floor and the blue coverlet on the bed matched the padded cushions on the straight-back chair.

"I'm sure I will, thank you."

Bolt turned around when he heard the door close. He was startled to see Mary standing in front of the door, unbuttoning the bodice of her red dress. Only a small portion of the soft breasts was exposed, but the sight of the bare flesh was enough to cause Bolt's loins to flood with heat.

"Bolt, will you make love to me?" she asked boldly, her blue eyes as innocent as a child's.

Chapter Four

Jack Ramsey held the reins loosely as he guided his horse, a big sorrel named Pete, down the steep rock-strewn incline at an angle. Sure-footed, the gelding picked its way through the thick mesquite bushes that jutted out from the sloping ground. Kyle Hutchinson's midnight-black horse, a young and frisky stallion, followed close behind.

From the slope, Ramsey couldn't see the small, protected meadow off to his right, where the Comanches were. And he knew they couldn't see him. The Indian camp was tucked away just beyond the horse-shoe bend in the river, hidden from Ramsey's view by the long green expanse of the trees, the dense cotton-woods and oaks that divided the valley into two separate meadows.

The Comanches were smart. They had chosen a spot to set up camp where they were totally secluded, where they wouldn't be seen unless someone wandered off the trail above them and looked down from the edge of the bluff, as Ramsey had done.

The rest of the tranquil valley, the part that he could see, was open, lush with tall grasses, dotted with low brush and the clumps of blue lupine. He squinted his eyes against the blinding glare of the stream where the afternoon sunlight reflected off the water's constantly-flowing surface. He tugged the brim of his Stetson down far enough for a ribbon of shade to cross his eyes. His gaze followed the tree-lined river as far as he could see it, until it disappeared between two bluffs off to his left. There were no Indian braves in sight.

Ramsey lurched in the saddle, grabbed the saddle-horn to steady himself when his horse stumbled on some loose rocks and almost lost his footing. Dust and pebbles kicked up as the sorrel raced down the last few feet of the slope and came to a stiff-legged stop at the bottom. Ramsey snapped the reins, spurred the animal on, and rode across the open meadow with Kyle Hutchinson right behind him. He kept the horse close to the edge of the stand of trees, using the thick foliage for cover. When he reached the river bend at the far side of the meadow, he reined up.

"You gonna leave the horses here and sneak up on them gals?" Hutch asked when he rode up beside Ramsey.

"No. We might need our horses. We'll ride on in and snatch 'em up quick. Get 'em while the gettin's good, then get the hell out."

Ramsey glanced down at the Remington .44 pistol that rode in the holster tied low around his leg. He reached down, tugged the Winchester .44 rifle a few inches out of the scabbard that dangled from leather thongs at the horse's right side. The rifle slid out smoothly. Satisfied that it wouldn't hang up on him if he needed it, he tapped the rifle back into the sling before he cracked the reins across Pete's shoulder.

As his horse found a path through the small, thick forest, Ramsey ducked his head, dodged the low branches that threatened to slap him across the face. Above the constant hum of the flowing river, he heard the creak of Hutch's saddle leather behind him as the two outlaws rode through the trees toward the Indian camp.

A cruel sense of satisfaction filled his twisted mind when he heard the happy chatter of the Indian girls beyond the trees. He was in full control of the girls' lives now, and he gloated over the fact that their happy chatter was soon to end.

When he came out on the other side of the trees, Ramsey stopped, help up a hand to caution his partner. The Indian maidens, who were talking and giggling, were not more than a hundred yards away. Both girls were squatting down with their backs to the outlaws and obviously hadn't sensed that anyone was behind them.

Ramsey glanced over at Hutch, nodded.

"You grab the one on your side," he whispered in a deep husk. "I'll get the other one." His jaw tightened. His eyes hardened to dark, cold stones. He dug his spurs into the sorrel, and with a quick, forward swing of his arm, gestured to move on.

The two outlaws rode down hard on the unsuspecting maidens and were within thirty feet of them when both girls suddenly spun around at the same time. The young girls stared up at the intruders, their innocent, fawn-like eyes wide with surprise.

For a brief instant, the two girls froze, awkward in their twisted, squatting positions. Their startled expressions were quickly shrouded with veils of horror when the riders continued to bear down on them. One girl's mouth fell open as if she were going to scream, but nothing came out.

The other maiden, the one whose Indian name meant Plover Egg, was the first to move. She scrambled to her feet and ran from the approaching horsemen.

Jack Ramsey headed straight for her.

Hutch jerked his reins to the left, bore down on the other frightened girl.

Little Killdeer jumped up and ran in a different direction.

Except for the patter of hoofbeats and the scuffling of soft moccasins on the hard ground, there was no sound in the camp. No sound to the girls' flailing arms, no sound to the tautened muscles in their fast-moving legs. No audible voice to their twin fears.

After a few steps, Little Killdeer glanced over her shoulder, a panic-stricken look on her face. Hutchinson was right behind her, ready to snatch her up. Desperate to get away from him, she stumbled, tripped over her own moccasins, fell to the ground. She clawed at the earth, pushed herself up, made low, guttural, grunting sounds in her frantic effort to regain her balance before the stranger could come and sweep her up.

From the saddle of his galloping horse, Hutch reached down for Little Killdeer. He missed his first attempt to capture the girl as his horse sped right on by her.

A few feet away, Jack Ramsey jabbed sharp spurs into Pete's side. The horse's hooves dug into the hard ground, spit up clumps of grass as the sorrel gained speed. Ramsey rode around in front of the fleeing Plover Egg, blocked her off from running toward the teepees.

Plover Egg switched directions with the agility and grace of a spooked deer and ran the other way.

Ramsey spun his horse around and chased her. Every time he got close enough to make a grab for Plover Egg, she dodged his grasp.

Little Killdeer managed to elude Kyle Hutchinson for a time. To escape the scar-faced outlaw's clutches, she ran around in tight figure-eight circles that forced

Hutch to constantly change the direction of his horse.

For a brief time, it was as if they were all playing some kind of an ancient game in which human animals, in the form of Indian maidens, would ultimately be sacrificed to their barbaric pursuers.

Ramsey enjoyed the chase, the feeling of invincible power that surged through him as he toyed with the girl as if she were a trapped rat. And when it came right down to the bare bones of the matter, he had about as much feeling and compassion for the Indian maiden as he would for the rat. Absolutely none at all. He knew he would be the ultimate victor, and intentionally allowed her to escape his grasp a few times, taking sadistic pleasure in seeing the fear in her doe-like eyes.

Knowing that he was totally in control of the situation, Ramsey jerked the reins, spun his horse around again, and headed back for Plover Egg, intending to take her captive this time. As he rode up on her, he leaned way out to the side and made a grab for her. He managed to snag her by the hair and held on tight. His horse came to an abrupt stop as Ramsey jerked the reins back.

Plover Egg's head snapped back as she was stopped in her tracks by the painful tug at one of her long braids. She caught her balance, struggled to free herself. Ramsey tightened his grip, pulled her hair harder. Finally, she reached back, grabbed the braid with both hands, and literally tore it away from her assailant.

Ramsey was surprised by the girl's strength, angered by his own humiliation. He glanced down at his hand, saw that it was empty except for a few strands of dark hair. He brought himself back up straight in the saddle, looked up in time to see the girl running away from him.

Enraged, Ramsey jumped down from his horse and

chased the girl down. He grabbed her by one arm, spun her around, dug his fingers into her tender flesh. The game was over. She wouldn't get away from him this time.

Plover Egg's scream pierced the tranquility of the peaceful meadow. The high-pitched wail echoed throughout the valley and seemed to linger for a long moment, like some primordial battle cry. The shrill outcry drove straight to Ramsey's eardrums and fanned the fires of his irrational, violent temper.

"Shut up," he snarled as he jerked her toward him. He slapped her hard across the face just as the two thick-waisted Indian squaws boiled out of their respective teepees and looked in his direction. The squaws stopped in their tracks when they saw the strangers.

Bright red welts blossomed on Plover Egg's bronze cheek where Ramsey had struck her. She batted back the tears that stung her eyes, but did not cry out again.

Ramsey cursed the fact that Plover Egg's scream had brought the squaws out. But he wasn't worried. They were only two fat women and there was nothing they could do to stop him from taking the young maidens.

The squaw who eyed them from the middle teepee was Chief Yellow Dog's woman, Picks Many Berries. She shook her arm at the intruders, shouted at them in her native tongue, a threatening tone to her loud, guttural words. She quickly ducked back inside her teepee.

The other squaw, who was called Dancing Bear, was Plover Egg's mother. She ran toward Ramsey and frantically hurled the small clay bowl that was in her hand at him, as if that would scare him away. The bowl crashed to the ground ten feet short of its mark and shattered as the squaw looked around for something else to throw.

"Dumb squaw," Ramsey laughed at the old woman.

He squeezed Plover Egg's arm tighter when the girl struggled to get away.

Kyle Hutchinson jumped down from his horse and overtook Little Killdeer. He grabbed her from behind, quickly clamped his hand over her mouth.

A small rock, snatched from the fire ring by Dancing Bear, hurtled toward Hutchinson's head. He ducked from its path, drew his pistol with his free hand, aimed it at the plump woman. Dancing Bear dropped the other rock she had picked up and half-ran, half-waddled back to the safety of her teepee.

Hutch jammed the pistol barrel against Little Killdeer's head and dragged her, arms flailing, to his horse.

Plover Egg screamed again. And the sound of it was like a hot needle searing into Ramsey's brain.

"You don't learn, do you, you little bitch?" He clapped his hand over her mouth, felt the delicate flesh of her cheeks give under his cruel roughness.

An instant later, pain seared through Ramsey when Plover Egg jerked her head around and bit down hard on the end of his forefinger. He let go of her arm, thinking, for a minute, that she'd bitten the entire tip of his finger off. He stared at the finger, saw the impressions of her teeth marks, but there was no blood.

"You goddamn bitch!" he shouted. "You'll pay for that!" He drew his arm back and drove a solid fist into her face. The loud thud of hard knuckles against the soft, pliable flesh of her cheek sounded like a dropped melon splitting open.

Plover Egg was staggered by the blow. She reeled back, tottered for a moment on shaky legs before she tumbled to the ground. Blood spurted from the cut on her high cheekbone, splattered across the front of her buckskin dress.

"Get up, you bitch," Ramsey ordered. He took a step

41

toward the girl as she started to crawl away, and was just about to reach down and jerk her to her feet when he saw a flash of colorful movement off to his right. He glanced that way and was startled to see Chief Yellow Dog standing in front of the middle teepee. The tall, gaunt Indian wore only a breechclout and Ramsey could see the rib bones beneath the wrinkled skin of the chief's bare chest. The chief's squaw peeked out at Ramsey from just inside the doorway where she held the flap of the teepee open with her chubby arm.

Ramsey's heart skipped a beat. The chief had seen him strike the maiden. He was sure of that. The withered old man held a bow in his outstretched hand, the arrow already set in place and pointed at Ramsey.

Damn, Ramsey thought. He hadn't counted on this kind of trouble. He'd been so sure that there weren't any Indian braves around the camp — not that this wrinkled old man who looked like he'd just risen from his deathbed could be called a brave.

But, no matter how frail he was, Chief Yellow Dog was still a mighty warrior. Ramsey could see it in the old man's cold, hard eyes as Chief Yellow Dog pulled the bowstring back, taut, and aimed the flint-tipped arrow directly at the outlaw's head.

Ramsey knew the swiftness of an Indian's arrow. And now, as he stared at the drawn bow, he could almost feel the sting of the arrowhead biting into his flesh. He could already feel the chill of death shivering up his spine and settling into his heart.

In the face of death, Jack Ramsey felt suddenly numb all over. For a fleeting moment, his arms seemed awkward, useless, his mind blank.

Still, he acted instinctively, not stopping to consider his chances against the old Indian chief. His muscles tightened, taut as Chief Yellow Dog's menacing bow-string.

Ramsey ducked down to his right, snagged his pistol out of its holster.

Chief Yellow Dog released the arrow at the same instant that Ramsey ducked. The thin, feathered shaft with its deadly-sharp flint arrowhead shot straight and true through the air, zinging toward Ramsey.

Beads of sweat popped out on Ramsey's forehead, trickled down into his eyes, momentarily blinding him as he blinked away the salty sting. Waiting for the arrow's bite, he cringed, held his breath. The arrow's whispered *hiss* flew by him, just beyond his ear.

The chief didn't hesitate, but reached back, withdrew another arrow from his quiver, quickly brought it around to the bow.

At the same time, Ramsey raised his pistol, thumbed back the hammer. He fired just as Chief Yellow Dog pulled the bowstring back for the second time.

The loud boom of the pistol shot shattered the tense silence, reverberated throughout the meadow.

Chief Yellow Dog caught the bullet high in his side, chest level, just as he released the second arrow. With the bowstring slightly slackened, there wasn't enough force behind the arrow to project it very far. It shot out straight for a short distance, then dropped to the ground, useless.

The chief made a grunting sound as the impact of the bullet knocked him backward, into the teepee, where his squaw watched with horror. Yellow Dog's hand clutched at his bare, bronzed chest. Inside that frail chest, the bullet had exploded his lungs. He gasped for breath, collapsed to the ground, his blood spilling out the neat hole in his side.

Picks Many Berries ducked out of the teepee, rushed over to her husband. She looked down at the chief, then glanced back at her daughter, Little Killdeer, who

43

had been captured by Hutch. She hesitated for a brief instant, as if trying to decide which one of her loved ones she should help. She stared at Little Killdeer's captor, a pleading look in her eyes, before she finally turned and kneeled down beside her husband.

Chief Yellow Dog looked up at his woman, tried to lift his head.

"It is . . . a good day . . . to die," he said, fighting for each precious breath as the pink, bloody foam spilled from his mouth. He gasped once more, clawed at his chest as if he were trying to open his breathing passages. And then his body went slack. His head rolled to the side and he stared up at the sky with sightless eyes.

Picks Many Berries clapped her hands to her face and let out a long, anguished moan. She leaned over Chief Yellow Dog and began chanting as she rocked back and forth on her knees. Dancing Bear rushed to the fallen chief's side where she kneeled down beside the man who had been her dead husband's only brother. She joined Picks Many Berries in the forlorn death chant.

Ramsey cursed his luck, cursed the squaws' monotonous, unnerving chant that range out across the meadow. He scanned the camp and was grateful that the loud shot had not brought braves running, but now that he'd killed the chief, he wanted to get the hell out of there before the Indians did return.

He grabbed Plover Egg by the leg as she tried to scamper away from him on her hands and knees. Gritty dirt and small pebbles scraped her leg, bit into her tender flesh as Ramsey dragged her toward him. He swung his pistol around, aimed it at her head.

"Get up, you piece of filth," he ordered. He let go of her leg, reached for her arm, and jerked her roughly to her feet. He hauled her over to his horse, who stood nearby, patiently flicking the pesky flies away with his tail. "Now, climb up there, girlie. You and me are goin' for a little ride."

"Not go with you," Plover Egg said in the white man's words she had learned from her brother. She stared up at Ramsey, but didn't budge. The flesh around her eye had already begun to swell and the cut on her cheekbone still oozed blood.

"Up, I said," Ramsey ordered again, patting the empty saddle.

Plover Egg's eyes shifted in their sockets as she glanced over at the other horse, the black stallion, where her cousin, Little Killdeer, and the ugly, scar-faced outlaw were jammed together in one saddle. The panic showed in Little Killdeer's eyes, but she couldn't speak. A white cloth gag was jammed into her mouth and tied at the back of her head.

Ramsey saw the girl's body begin to tremble, but he didn't give a damn about her stupid fears. He shoved the gun up against her forehead.

"Now, get your ass up in that saddle!" he ordered.

Plover Egg opened her mouth to scream. "*Ahhh—*" was all she got out when Ramsey brought the pistol back and smashed it against her cheek. Her head reeled back. "Ohhhh," she moaned. She lowered her head and brought her hands up to the fresh wound.

"You ain't learned yet, have ya?" Ramsey bellowed. He jammed his pistol in the holster, whipped out his red bandanna. She fought him with her hands, but he managed to cover her mouth with it and wrap it around her head. He pulled it tight, until it bit into her flesh, then tied a quick knot.

"Now, get up there," he ordered again.

The girl turned and tried awkwardly to mount the horse. Ramsey grabbed her by the butt and shoved her on up into the saddle.

Plover Egg screamed with all her might, but the sound was muffled through the cloth and didn't carry very far.

Ramsey was furious. He pulled himself up and settled in behind her.

"You don't make any more noise at all or I'll whop your damned head off," Ramsey warned her. "You understand that, girlie?"

Plover Egg's body stiffened. She gave a slight nod of her head.

"Good. Let's go," he called to Hutch.

The monotonous chanting of the two grieving Indian squaws continued as Ramsey reached around Plover Egg's rigid body and grabbed the reins. He jabbed sharp spurs into the horse's flanks, headed the sorrel toward the wide stand of oaks and cottonwoods near the river bend.

Jack Ramsey glanced back at the camp just before he rode into the thick foliage of the trees. His chest swelled with satisfaction when he saw the two squaws still rocking back and forth and chanting their prayers over the dead Comanche chief. Ramsey had been right all along. There were no Indian braves at the Comanche camp that morning, after all.

Ramsey felt mighty smug, mighty powerful as he guided his horse through the thick trees. He and Hutch had been successful in capturing the girls, and as soon as they got through the trees and reached the other part of the quiet meadow, they would have a clear shot back up to the road where they would soon catch up to the other outlaws. The rest of his plan to seek revenge against Bolt was going to be easy.

Almost too easy.

Chapter Five

Gray Wolf was not in any particular hurry that warm August afternoon. There was no need to hurry. The other members of the hunting party traveled much slower and were far behind him. Soon he would ride into his own camp, happy that he carried the good news. The hunt had been successful and his tribe would not want for food.

He rode tall and proud on his unshod Indian pony, with only a blanket under him to make his ride more comfortable. The colorful blanket, he knew, carried the luck of the gods and he was grateful for it. The blanket was special to him because it had been woven for him by his mother, Dancing Bear, and his sister, Plover Egg, and presented to him on his Day Of Becoming A Man.

But he did not think about such things on this good warm day. He did not even think about the time when he would become chief of his Comanche tribe, which he knew would happen before many more moons passed.

Gray Wolf's uncle, Chief Yellow Dog, was very old and so ill he could not eat anything except the special broth his wife prepared for him with the secret herbs that she kept in her precious medicine pouch. But the herbs did little good and Yellow Dog became weaker with each passing sun. And because Gray Wolf had proven his bravery during the many wars with other tribes, he'd been chosen to succeed Yellow Dog as the leader of the tribe.

It was the first time that the small tribe had not journeyed together on a hunt. Chief Yellow Dog had been too ill to accompany them, and they had left the two squaws and the two maidens in camp to take care of him.

The Indian scout did not wear the red and black war paint this day. This had not been a journey to make war on other tribes. In the heat, he wore only a fringed breechclout to cover his nakedness and sturdy moccasins on his feet. His beaded, brain-tanned, buckskin bow case and quiver were attached to the wide leather thong that was slung over his shoulder. His old rifle and his trusty tomahawk rode in separate sheaths that hung from thongs at his pony's sides.

Around his neck, he wore the symbol of his bravery, a necklace fashioned from bear teeth and curved bear claws, intermingled with colorful beads.

The two eagle feathers that stuck out from his long black hair would all too soon be replaced by the full-feathered war bonnet that now belonged to the uncle he loved so much. Gray Wolf's own father had died in battle when Gray Wolf had been but ten years old. Since that time, his father's brother, Chief Yellow Dog, had raised Gray Wolf as if he were his own son, sharing his special wisdom with the boy, teaching Gray Wolf to be a brave warrior and an honorable tribesman. It would be a sad day when the chief's feathered headpiece was placed on Gray Wolf's head.

As scout for the hunting expedition, Gray Wolf rode alone, many hoofbeats ahead of the other braves who carried the rewards of the hunt back to camp. His heart was glad this day, because the hunt had been successful and soon he could tell his people that they would have much buffalo and antelope meat to fill the pots instead of the fish they had been eating for so long.

The plentiful bounty from the hunt. And the happy faces of his people when they saw the bounty. These were the things Gray Wolf was thinking about when the muffled sound of the distant scream came to his ears.

He reined the spotted poney to a halt, cocked his head and listened. He heard nothing but the breeze singing in the trees, the gurgling water of the river he followed back to camp. He was still some distance from his camp, but he thought the high-pitched wail had come from that direction. Had it only been a coyote's howl? Or perhaps the screech of a nearby owl? Were his usually keen ears playing tricks on him on this very good day?

After focusing his senses on the sounds in the air for a few minutes, Gray Wolf touched the heel of his moccasin to his pony's side and rode on. A short time later, the shrill scream came to his ears again.

His heart jumped and tumbled into his stomach. Yes, it was the scream of a woman that floated to him on the gentle afternoon breezes. He was sure of it this time. He stiffened, suddenly chilled by the sense of foreboding that stabbed at his heart, the helplessness he felt at being yet so far from camp. He was near the twin meadows now and knew that the scream came from the place where the teepees stood. Knowing that trouble had come to his camp this day, he snapped the reins. The pony responded to his command and picked up speed.

A shot rang out just as Gray Wolf reached the peaceful meadow where the lupines grew tall. He wished for his spirit to speed to the bend in the river and fly over the stand of trees to his people. But, in his heart, he already knew that there was tragedy in the camp. He flicked the reins across the pony's shoulder, pressed his moccasin deeper into the animal's side. The horse dug its hooves into the ground and shot across the open meadow, heading straight for the trees that blocked Gray Wolf's view of the camp.

Gray Wolf, who did not know fear in the face of battle, felt frightened for the first time in his twenty-three years and he did not understand how butterflies could dance in his stomach. He did not fear for himself, but for those of his tribe, the women they had left at the camp. He feared most for his mother, Dancing Bear, and his sister, Plover Egg. And he feared for his beloved uncle, Chief Yellow Dog, who would fight with his dying breath to protect the members of his tribe.

He hauled back on his pony when he reached the bend in the river where the trees grew thick. That's when the other sounds fell on his ears. The snapping of twigs and the padding of slow hoofbeats signalled the presence of a horse in the woods. Two horses, he decided, after listening more carefully. Those kind of noises had become familiar to him as the braves of his tribe had traveled to and from the camp during the short time they'd been settled there. But the other sounds, the low, muffled voices that floated through the trees, were strange to his ears.

He tried to peer into the woods, but his vision could not penetrate the thick foliage. He sniffed the air and smelled the faint odor of sweat that hung in the air. Strong, rancid sweat that could only come from a white man's skin.

His stomach knotted with anger. He wanted to rush into the woods and kill the white men who had intruded on the privacy of his people. But Chief Yellow

Dog had taught him the meaning of caution. And the benefit of surprise. Yes, it would be better to wait there and surprise the white men when they came out of the woods.

He slid off his pony, pulled his tomahawk from its case, and stuck the deadly weapon in the strap of his breechclout. He slapped the pony across its rear, pointed toward the row of trees that lined the river a short distance away from him. The horse obeyed his silent command and trotted over to the covering of the trees where he would wait patiently for his owner to call him back.

Without making a sound, the Comanche scout stepped over to a thick-trunked oak at the edge of the woods. He pressed his back up against the rough bark, so close to the tree that he didn't cast a shadow of his own on the ground. He reached over his shoulder, brought his bow out of its buckskin case, then tugged an arrow from the quiver and held it near the bow.

Gray Wolf was ready for the strangers who had brought trouble to his camp on this day, the happiest day of the hunt.

Although the sound of muffled voices had stopped, the distinct noise of snapping twigs grew louder, along with the crunching of dead, brittle leaves under the horses' hooves. And then the Indian saw the shadowy movement through the trees. He saw glimpses of brown and white, a brief flash of red, but not well enough to distinguish any particular figures. The white eyes were getting closer. Soon they would emerge from the woods and come into view.

Gray Wolf set the arrow to the bow and waited. He would not raise the bow, nor pull the bowstring back until he was ready. That was something he'd learned from Chief Yellow Dog. If he stretched his bowstring back too soon and then waited, his aim would not be true.

"I told you it'd be as easy as plunkin' rocks against the side of an elephant," Ramsey's deep, raspy voice echoed out from the forest.

"We're not out of the woods yet," Hutch said. "That shot you fired back there is likely to bring the redskins flocking in here from miles around."

"Couldn't be helped. We'll just keep an eye on our backtrail."

Still, Gray Wolf could not see the horsemen. He cocked his head, listened intently. Using his keen sense of hearing, he zeroed in on their position in the trees. They would emerge from the woods some twenty-five yards to his left. He eased around to the side of the tree and faced the spot where they would soon appear.

"Are you gonna head straight for Cow Town and Bolt's ranch?" Hutch asked.

"Yep. Stoppin' only long enough to do some funnin' with the gals." Ramsey's gravel voice answered.

Gray Wolf's heart raced when he saw the blur of colors in the woods, the glimpses of movement beyond the tree leaves. Nearer the ground, where there was no foliage around the tree trunks to block his view, he spotted the advancing horses's legs. Five of them, he counted, but knew there were eight. He had figured right on the distance. He knew he had only seconds to wait.

Instead of tensing up, he felt a calmness come over him, the calmness that came from knowing what he had to do and being ready to follow through. Chief Yellow Dog had taught him well. He brought the bow and arrow up, shoulder high. He held the bow out at arm's length, sighted in on the spot where the riders would appear. He was prepared to fire the first arrow and grab another for the second horseman.

Poised, he began the count. Five . . . Four . . .

Three — he pulled the bowstring and arrow back with a sure, steady pressure — Two . . . One.

His timing was perfect. At the count of one, the horses broke out of the woods and came into the clearing. He started to release the arrow, but just in time, his fingers clamped tight around the shaft of the arrow to keep it in place.

The stranger had Plover Egg!

Gray Wolf's heart fluttered wildly in his chest when he saw his sister on the horse with the tall, vicious white man. A dozen ropes seemed to knot together in his stomach when he saw the red cloth that bound Plover Egg's mouth, and the bruises on her face. Even from that distance, he could see the cruelty in the dark eyes of the man who crowded himself up against poor, little Plover Egg.

His anguish was doubled when the second horse appeared and he saw Little Killdeer huddled in front of the other ugly white man.

Gray Wolf let the bowstring slacken slightly as the shock of the situation settled into him. His nostrils flared with anger. His jaw stiffened and his eyes became dark slits of hatred. He wanted revenge. Immediate reprisal against his sister's and little Killdeer's captors. He felt suddenly helpless, though, with his bow and arrow. He couldn't risk Plover Egg's life by shooting from such a distance. Or Little Killdeer's.

The wise words of Chief Yellow Dog came to him then: "The greater the crisis, the greater the need to remain calm." Gray Wolf stood still, contemplating a course of action, and wished he was still on his pony where he could get to his old rifle.

Plover Egg's head turned as she looked around. She quickly spotted gray Wolf by the tree and he could see the look of fright in her expression, the pleading in her eyes. She threw herself forward, leaned down flat, as close as she could against the horse, giving her brother a better shot with the bow and arrow.

Gray Wolf always shot a true arrow, but this time he hesitated. The horses were moving and it was still too risky to shoot.

Plover Egg's sudden plunge forward caused Jack Ramsey to become alarmed. He scanned the meadow with a quick swing of his head and it took him only an instant to discover the Indian who stood by the tree.

"Stop!" Gray Wolf shouted when he saw the stranger staring at him. He raised his bow and arrow. "You not take my sister or Little Killdeer."

Ramsey jerked the reins, turned his horse to face the Indian. He switched the reins to his left hand, snagged his pistol out of its holster with his right hand, and headed straight for Gray Wolf.

"We take your women for the whorehouse, Injun," he sneered as he neared the Indian. "They are virgins, are they not?"

"I will kill you, bastard!" Gary Wolf said. He started to tug the bowstring back, but let it go slack.

Ramsey reined up a few yards from the Indian. "Ha, you must be Gray Wolf," he said as he thumbed back the hammer of his pistol.

"They call me Gray Wolf. Let my sister go."

"They call me Bolt," Ramsey lied. "I hear you're brave and cruel, but that don't scare me none. We need your pretty maidens. They will be playthings for the rough, dirty men who come to the bordello," he taunted.

"I kill you before you take my sister." Gray Wolf jerked the bowstring back, aimed the arrow at a spot between Ramsey's eyes.

Ramsey dropped the reins, grabbed Plover Egg by the braid, and jerked her back to a sitting position in front of him.

"Go ahead and shoot, Injun, but your sister will take your arrow and die. Let's see how brave and cruel you are now."

Once again the bowstring went slack. Gray Wolf saw the frightened look in his sister's eyes. He couldn't risk it and he hated the white man for knowing that.

Ramsey leveled his pistol at the Indian's face. He fired just as Gray Wolf ducked behind the thick trunk of the oak tree. The bullet ripped through the side of the tree and chipped off chunks of bark.

An instant later, Gray Wolf leaned his head out, peered around the tree. He saw the horse riding away. "Stop!" he called, but then, out of the corner of his eye, he saw the movement. He glanced back over his shoulder and saw the man with Little Killdeer riding his way, pistol drawn. Gray Wolf ducked again.

A second explosion cracked the air as Kyle Hutchinson fired from farther away. The shot was short and the bullet tore into the ground a few feet from its mark.

Ramsey turned his horse around and bore down on the Indian again.

Gray Wolf raised the bow, drew the bowstring back, and with a flick of his fingers, let the arrow go. The shaft whispered through the air and plowed the ground a few feet in front of the charging horse, just as Gray Wolf had planned.

The horse spooked. It whinnied and bucked, pawing the air with its hooves.

Plover Egg was thrown about, but managed to grab the horse's mane and hang on.

Gray Wolf watched the big man tip back and hoped he would fall off the backside of the horse. But the white man kept his balance until the horse brought its feet back to the ground and wheeled around.

Gray Wolf quickly plucked a second arrow from his quiver. He brought his bow up, led the horse, aimed the arrow ahead of the animal. Again, the shaft plowed into the ground in the horse's path. The sorrel shied away from it, changed directions, pranced around in a frantic circle. The Comanche scout whirled around and sent another arrow flying toward the flanks of Hutchinson's black stallion, stopping the animal in its tracks. He quickly fired a second arrow in that direction. The dark horse pivoted and galloped off toward the trees.

With Plover Egg settled in front of him again, Ramsey fumbled with the reins. He gained control of his horse and charged the Indian.

Plover Egg acted quickly. She brought her arms up, slammed her elbow back against Ramsey's wrist.

"Bitch!" Ramsey yelled as the pistol tumbled from his hand and slammed to the ground. He brought his empty hand around and slapped Plover Egg hard across the side of her head.

Gray Wolf saw the vicious man his his sister. Enraged, he dropped his bow to the ground, snatched the tomahawk out of the strap of his breechclout, and ran toward the charging horse.

Ramsey leaned over, snagged his rifle out of its sheath, but not in time to do him any good.

Gray Wolf side-stepped out of the horse's path. As the horse passed him, the Indian brought the tomahawk down and slashed at Ramsey's leg.

Ramsey screamed. He tried to hit Gray Wolf with the butt of his rifle, but missed.

Gray Wolf saw the crimson stain blossom and spread over the man's pant leg. It wasn't the disabling blow he'd wanted, but at least he'd drawn blood with his tomahawk.

Ramsey worked his horse, chased after Gray Wolf, tried to run him down.

Plover Egg screamed, but it was muffled.

Gray Wolf ran a few feet, changed directions, darted back toward the trees, then changed directions again, avoiding the horse with each pass that Ramsey made. Finally, when the horse was close behind him, Gray Wolf stopped dead in his tracks, turned to face his approaching enemy. He raised his tomahawk, prepared to strike another blow.

"Aaeeiii! Aaeeiii!" he shouted as the horse approached. At the last minute, he realized that Ramsey's leg was too close to Plover Egg's leg for him to slash out with the tomahawk. He hesitated, and knew he'd lost his advantage.

The horse bore down on him. He saw the stranger swing the rifle toward him. Gray Wolf raised his arm higher, tried to ward off the blow. The butt of the rifle slammed into his arm. Pain shot through his wrist, coursed up through his arm. He fought to keep his grip on the tomahawk, but the blow jarred it loose from his hand. The weapon clattered to the ground, useless.

As the horse fled on by, Gray Wolf ignored the pain, stooped over to retrieve the tomahawk. As he stood up, the man and beast were on him again.

He saw the cruel expression on the stranger's face as the wicked man swung the rifle toward his head.

Gray Wolf tried to duck, but was too late. When the rifle butt smashed against the side of his head, it felt like his skull shattered in a thousand pieces. His knees buckled and he started to go down.

"Kill him!" he heard the other kidnapper shout from somewhere in the hazy distance.

"No! Gray Wolf will live to remember what we have done to his women."

Gray Wolf felt as if he were being sucked into a deep, dark tunnel. As he tumbled, he saw only the ugly face of the rough man who called himself Bolt. His ears heard only the raspy, ringing voices of the men who carried Plover Egg and Little Killdeer away.

To Gray Wolf, it seemed as if he floated forever in that dark tunnel, until he finally hit the hard ground. A black cloud closed in around his mind and blotted out all memory.

Chapter Six

Pain throbbed through Ramsey's leg as he sped across the meadow with the Indian maiden huddled in front of him on the big sorrel. He leaned out to the side, glanced down, and saw the crimson stain that spread out in a circle from the rip in his trousers. The slash wound was on the side of his leg, about four inches below the knee.

The stain was as big as a dinner plate, but it didn't seem to be spreading any bigger. At least the bleeding had stopped. He hoped it wouldn't start up again; he didn't have time to mess with it right then. He just wanted to get the hell out of there before the other Indian braves returned to camp.

Kyle Hutchinson's black stallion followed on the heels of Ramsey's horse as they made their way back up to the road. The Indian girls rode stiff and still in front of their captors, and Ramsey and Hutch didn't speak again until they met up with the five other members of the outlaw group who waited for them up the road a piece, under the shade of three big oak trees.

Young Vernon Tate was the first one to spot them. He was the only one who was still on his horse. The others were stretched out under the oaks, using the tree trunks for backrests.

"Here they come now," he called out. "And they've got the girls."

"Really? They got Little Killdeer?" Fester Grodin smiled. He flicked his burning cigarette onto the bare ground where he'd already tossed three others, and stood up. He brushed the dirt from the seat of his pants, straightened his vest, and looked down the road.

Zeke Wiley got up and stretched his stiff muscles as he walked over to Fess Grodin. He scratched the stubble of whiskers on his pockmarked face.

"They got Plover Egg, too?" Big Mac Sloan asked. With all the weight he carried, he had more trouble pulling himself up.

Oppie Shenker picked up his flask, which was on the ground beside him, and stuffed it into his waistband. When the outlaws had first stopped there to wait for Ramsey and Hutch, Oppie had filled the flask from one of the bottles he carried in his saddlebags. Now the container was almost empty. When he stood up, he had to reach out and grab the tree trunk to keep his balance. He'd always been a hard-drinking man, but lately, the whiskey seemed to hit him harder. This time he blamed it on the heat.

He staggered slightly as he strolled over to his horse. The other men were facing the road and didn't notice. He put the flask to his lips, tipped it back, and emptied it before he put it away in his saddlebag. He wasn't worried. He never drank when they were pulling a robbery and they weren't really working today. It was a day when they'd all have their turn at the Indian maidens.

"Mount up, men," Ramsey called from twenty yards away. "We gotta keep moving."

"We heard the shot. What happened?" Tate asked as Ramsey reined up in front of him.

"I killed their chief."

"What happened to your leg?"

"Gray Wolf came back early and tried to take a chunk out of my leg."

"Did you kill him, too?" asked Zeke Wiley as he walked over closer.

"I don't think so. I think I just knocked him out cold." Pain shot up Ramsey's leg. He leaned over and saw that the bloodstain had spread into a wider circle and below the wound his pantleg was drenched with blood. He touched a spot well above the gash and winced. The pain was almost unbearable. "Think one of you men are going to have to take the girl."

"I'll take her," Big Mac Sloan grinned, his eyes glittering with lust.

Hutch laughed. "I hardly think she'll fit on your horse with you, Slim Sloan."

"What d'ya mean?" Sloan objected. "I wouldn't mind at all cozyin' up real close to Plover Egg."

"Ha," Hutch said. "If she rode with you, your prick would swell up like a summer squash and you'd have no place to put it."

"The hell I wouldn't," Sloan countered. "She could sit on my lap and I'd jam it up her slot. It'd feel real good having her bounce up and down on it while we're riding along."

"You ain't got no lap," Fester Grodin said.

Sloan stepped over closer to Ramsey's horse and looked up at the frightened girl. "You remember me, don't you, girly?" he said as he reached up and squeezed Plover Egg's thigh.

Plover Egg jerked back.

"Back off, Sloan," Ramsey warned. "You'll have plenty of time for that later."

"I'll carry the girl with me," Zeke Wiley offered. "But first, I think we should take a look at your leg, Ram. Looks like you've lost a lot of blood."

"Yeah, dammit, I thought the bleeding had stopped I guess I should have taken care of it back there, but could almost smell those Indians coming up on us. just wanted to get the hell out of there."

"Did you see any other Indians?" Zeke said as h tried to lift Ramsey's pantleg so he could check th wound.

"Oooooh," he winced. "That hurts. No, I think Gra Wolf was the scout. But you know damned well th others'll be there soon, and it won't take 'em long to ge up a war party."

Zeke looked around. "Come here, Tate, help me ge this gal down."

"Take those damned gags out of their mouths, Ramsey ordered. "If either one of them makes a noise knock 'em in the head."

Tate dismounted, and with a little help from Ramsey, he and Zeke pulled the girl down from Ramsey saddle.

"Put her on my horse, and keep your eye on her unti I'm through here," Zeke said.

"Oh, I'll watch her," Tate said as he led the girl away.

Fess Grodin walked over to Hutchinson's horse "You want her to ride with me for a spell?" he aske Hutch, nodding toward Little Killdeer.

"Yeah, go ahead." Hutch helped get the Indian gir down, then dismounted and walked over to look a Ramsey's leg.

Zeke tugged his knife out of its sheath, then gentl pulled on the bottom of Ramsey's pantleg. "We'r gonna have to cut your pants a little," he said.

Ramsey winced. "Go ahead. Cut the whole damned leg off if you want to."

Hutch reached over and held the bloody fabric out a Zeke cut a long slit in the pantleg. Once that was done and Zeke had put the knife away, Hutch held the material away from the wound so Zeke could examine it.

"Not as bad as I thought it'd be," Zeke announced after a minute. He looked up at Ramsey, who was still on his horse. "The gash is about two inches long, but it isn't very deep. If we can keep it from bleeding any more, you'll be all right until you can get to a doctor."

"I ain't goin' to no sawbones," Ramsey grumbled. "Just tie it up the best you can."

Zeke went over to his horse and dug a piece of neatly folded white cloth out of the medicine pouch he carried in his saddlebag. He unfolded it and tore a long, two-inch strip and two shorter, half-inch strips off the clean cloth. He covered the gash, then wrapped the strips around Ramsey's leg several times and tied it off. He tied a narrower strip around the leg, above the wound, just tight enough to serve as a tourniquet. Then, while Hutch pulled the bloody pantleg back over the bandage, Zeke tied another narrow strip around the bottom of the pantleg to keep the road dust from getting inside the trousers.

"You finished?" Ramsey asked.

"Yeah, I pinched the sides of the split flesh together, so maybe it'll heal itself over if you don't bang it against something and break it open again."

"Thanks, Zeke. Let's get moving, men. We'll stop and rest the horses in about an hour."

"When do we get the girls?" Sloan asked.

"Not until we get close to Bolt's place," Ramsey answered. He cracked his reins and his horse started out ahead of the others. A few minutes later, Hutch rode up beside him.

"You still think the Indians are gonna go after Bolt's hide?" Hutch asked.

"Yes." Ramsey stared straight ahead, the look in his eyes as hard and cold as a frozen winter pond. "I don't think Bolt will live long enough to see the sun rise in the morning."

Bolt was startled by the girl's boldness. He wondered if Mary Beth Piker had any idea what she was getting herself into by asking such a question.

He smiled at her, stepped closer, and took her hands in his to keep her from unbuttoning any more of the small, cloth-covered buttons of her long red dress.

"It just doesn't happen that way, Mary," Bolt said in a gentle voice.

"Yes, it does. Aunt Millie told me that when two people wanted each other, they went to bed together and made love, with no feelings of guilt about it. She said it was a natural thing between a man and a woman, to want each other that way."

"That's true, but . . ."

"Well, I want you, Bolt," she pleaded.

"Look, Mary, when two people make love, it has to be because they have a special feeling about each other, because they really care about each other. We just met. We barely know each other."

"You don't want me, do you, Bolt?" she pouted. "Why don't you just come right out with it?"

"It isn't that, Mary. As a matter of fact, I find you very attractive." He stepped back, held her arms out, and studied her face. "You're a pretty girl, Mary," he smiled. "And you're very desirable. Under different circumstances, maybe . . ."

"You slept with Aunt Millie when you were in Fort Worth, didn't you?" she accused. She jerked her hands back, turned her head away from him.

"A gentleman doesn't tell. Besides, that doesn't have anything to do with us, Mary."

"You only knew Aunt Millie a couple of days and

you made love to her. I know you did by the way she acted all giddy when we talked about you. So, I don't see what the difference is," she challenged as she looked him straight in the eye.

"Making love for the first time is an important step for a woman. Whether it's good or whether it's bad, it can affect her relationships with men for the rest of her life. I just don't want you to do anything that you'd regret later."

"I wouldn't regret it, but it's quite obvious that you would. Good-bye, Mr. Bolt." She stormed across the room, jerked the hatpins out of her hair, and plunked the red hat down on the dresser. She glanced into the gilded mirror in front of her, quickly buttoned the undone buttons of her dress, then fluffed her blond curls.

Bolt stared at her back for a moment, tempted to just walk out and let her sulk. But the girl had come a long way to see him and he felt obliged to stay and clear up their misunderstandings. He strolled across the room, stood a few feet behind her. He removed his Stetson, toyed with the brim, tried to find the right words.

"Mary, I'm sorry we got off on the wrong foot. I know you're tired from the long trip and . . ."

She whirled around and glared at him

"Don't tell me I'm tired, Mr. Bolt," she snapped. "I feel fine. In fact, the stage driver allowed for a stopover last night at his sister's ranch just north of here. As it turned out, his sister owns a small mansion and I had a hearty meal, a long, luxurious bath, and I got a good night's sleep in a big, comfortable bed. So I feel quite rested today."

"I'm glad. Riding in a stage can wear you to a frazzle."

The expression on Mary's face softened. "You rejected me, Mr. Bolt, and I accept it. It's that simple. Now please go and leave me alone."

Bolt looked into her eyes and saw the hurt that she tried to hide with her nonchalant attitude. He took a deep breath and smelled her heady scent.

"But I didn't reject you. You're a very lovely girl and I'd be pleased to share your bed. I just don't think you really want that."

"Please don't patronize me, Mr. Bolt. Don't call me a girl and don't tell me what I want and don't want," she flared.

"Do you think that sleeping with a man is going to make a woman out of you?" he said, his patience wearing thin. "Maybe that's the way you gals think, I don't know. But as far as I'm concerned, you're already a woman and I'd be plumb crazy if I didn't want to sleep with you. It's your feelings I'm thinking of, but you don't seem to understand what I'm trying to say."

"Oh, I understand you perfectly well," she answered, a stubborn tone to her frenzied voice. "It must be nice having those harlots working for you. Whenever you get the urge, you can just snap your fingers and have a warm body in bed with you. And all for free. You must be the envy of every man in town. So, yes, I can understand why you don't want to bother with me."

"Pettiness doesn't become you," he said, trying not to let his irritation show. He could understand why she felt rejected, but he didn't like jealous women.

"Neither does being a virgin, apparently."

She turned her head away and Bolt saw that she was about to break into tears. He wanted to take her in his arms and assure her that she was a pretty girl and a very likable person. But he'd already told her these things and it didn't seem to matter to her. He just figured he'd never understand women. He didn't know what to say next, so he just stood there with his hat in his hand.

After a minute of staring down at the floor, Mary took a deep breath, then looked at him. Bolt saw that she was tense, rigid.

"I'm sorry, Bolt. I guess I'm more tired from the trip than I thought I was. I'm really not myself."

"Well, if it matters to you," he said gently, "I don't sleep with the girls who work for me."

"Oh? Another one of your rules?"

He ignored her sarcasm.

"Yep. I don't mix business with pleasure."

He saw the taut muscles in her face relax and knew that she was secretly pleased.

"Well, it really doesn't matter," she sighed. "I knew from the beginning that you didn't want to hire me. And since I've wasted enough of your time already, I won't trouble you any more." She smiled and offered her hand. "Thanks for meeting the stage."

Bolt took her hand, then, impulsively, leaned forward and kissed her briefly on the lips.

"Will you have supper with me this evening, Miss Piper?" he beamed.

"No thank you, Mr. Bolt. You've done enough for me already."

Bolt shoved his hat on his head, turned, and started for the door. He'd coddled her enough and he wouldn't get down on his knees and beg her to go to dinner with him, if that's what she was looking for. He glanced back over his shoulder at her.

"You're bull-headed, Miss Piper. You know that?"

"Crudely put, but you're right," she said. "Sometimes I'm too stubborn for my own good."

"And this is one of those times. Well, play the martyr if you want to, but I won't beg."

"Bolt," she called as he reached for the doorknob.

"Yeah?"

"I'd be pleased to have supper with you tonight. I was really trying to be considerate of you, but I guess it didn't come across that way. I thought you had to get right back out to the ranch."

"That can wait," he smiled, as he let go of the doorknob.

"Can you give me a few minutes to wash up and change into a clean dress?"

"You need some help?"

"No, I'm quite capable of dressing myself, thank you."

"I'm sure you are," Bolt laughed. He pulled his gold pocket watch out of his pocket and checked the time. "Hmmm, it's only four o'clock. A little early for dinner. Do you want to wait and eat a little later?"

"Yes, let's eat later. Do you know what I'd really like to do?"

"What's that?"

"It's such a nice afternoon, I'd like to take a stroll around town before we eat so I can see a little of San Antonio. If you wouldn't mind."

"I'd be pleased to show you around."

"Good. It'd be a shame to go back to Fort Worth without seeing the Alamo. The stage driver's sister told us a lot about the Alamo last night. Her husband's father was one of the men who died in the battle."

"Yeah, I think you should see it. I've walked around the Alamo, and even after all these years, I swore I could still smell the gunpowder. I'll be back in about fifteen minutes. Will that give you enough time?"

"I'll hurry."

Bolt walked down to the dining room and made dinner reservations for five-thirty, figuring it would take that long to show her around town. And then, to kill a little time, he went to the hotel saloon and sipped a drink of whiskey. When he thought he'd given her plenty of time to change clothes, he returned to Mary's room and tapped on the door.

Mary was wearing a long, blue velvet robe when she opened the door. The robe was parted slightly in front and Bolt saw that she wore nothing under it. He saw just a glimpse of her bare breasts, but it was enough to know that they were firm and nicely rounded.

"Looks like I didn't give you enough time," he said. He avoided looking down at her thighs where the robe was parted even more.

"Not quite. But come in. You can look the other way while I dress, can't you?"

"It won't be easy," he teased as he stepped into the room.

Mary closed the door, then turned and faced him. He smelled the scent of her fresh perfume and his knees felt weak. She looked into his eyes for a long time, so long that Bolt became uncomfortable. He shifted his weight to the other foot, but did not look away from her. He didn't trust himself to look anywhere else.

He saw the expression in her eyes, the hunger for love, the need for understanding, the desire, and he tried to ignore all of it. He felt the fiery sparks that passed between them and melted inside.

"You know, Bolt, I've been thinking about you while you've been gone," she said, finally. "You really are a gentleman."

"I've been called worse," he said, trying to make light of the situation.

"No, I mean it, Bolt. Most men would have taken advantage of me, I suppose, but I admire you for not trying to . . . well, you know, for treating me like a lady. Thank you."

Before Bolt could speak, she stood on tiptoes, wrapped her arms around his neck, and gave him what started out to be a quick, friendly kiss. She started to back away, but lingered there for a moment with their lips just barely apart. Then she put her lips on his again and they were soft and warm and passionate.

As she kissed him, she snuggled in closer and slowly, sensually, thrust her body up tight against him. He felt the heat of her passion, felt the warmth that flooded his own loins.

He put his arms around her waist, drew her even closer, kissed her hard, suddenly full of his own needs, his own passion.

She broke the kiss, finally, and took a deep breath.

"I want you, Bolt," she said, her voice full of the husk that comes with desire. "I want you more than anything I've ever wanted in my life."

"Say things like that and you may not think me a gentleman much longer."

"Please, Bolt. I want you."

And Bolt knew he couldn't turn her down.

Chapter Seven

In his land of sleeping thoughts, Gray Wolf dreamed of the time when the Season Of The Cold Winds Blowing would come and his small tribe would journey south where they would live among other Comanche tribes in their winter camp. He did not dream of the cold nights that would come with the season, but rather of the blazing campfires that would keep them warm, and of the sweat lodge. He dreamed of his faraway sweetheart, Yellow Rose Bud, and felt the heat of her love wash across his body.

Even though he dreamed of these good times to come, his sleep-visions were filled with threads of frustration. The ghostly face of an evil white man seemed to drift down from the sky and hover above him, but vanished before he could reach out and grab it.

In his dream, his sister's muffled cry for help floated all around him. He felt the nagging urge to go and find her, but could not force his muscles to move. And once, Plover Egg appeared before him for a brief beat of the heart before she was slowly pulled back away from him. It was as if a giant, invisible wind god had swept down and snatched her up. She kicked her legs and flailed her arms, reached out to him. He tried frantically to chase after her and snatch her back from the evil wind god, but his feet were trapped in a mire of mud. Some unseen spirit dragged her further and further away from him. He saw her gasp for air, as if the wind god had strangled her with vicious, invisible hands. And just before she vanished completely, he saw her glare at him, her doe eyes full of accusation. He felt guilty. He felt helpless.

When she was gone, another vision came to him in the form of arms, bare and bronze, and not connected to anything. The dozen pairs of muscled arms carried Chief Yellow Dog's ceremonial war bonnet to him and tried to place it on his head. But the colorful headdress, with its many feathers of honor, was too heavy, and Gray Wolf pushed it away.

These were the frustrating threats that dangled throughout his sleeping thoughts, threads that he could not weave together into anything he could make sense of in his sleeplike state.

Gray Wolf awoke to the sound of familiar voices. The smell of summer grasses and fresh earth, the heavy aroma of horseflesh, were strong in his nostrils. His mouth was dry, his throat parched. He felt hot all over, as if he'd been roasted on a spit over an open fire, and yet, he was chilled by the warm summer breeze.

His eyelids fluttered, then blinked open. He recognized the cluster of bronze-skinned braves who stood over him, their black-haired braids gleaming in the late afternoon sunlight. His friends' arms looked distended as they reached down for him and for a minute he thought he was still dreaming.

"He is alive!" shouted one of the braves.

Gray Wolf knew he was lying flat on the hard ground, but didn't know where he was. He glanced around, tried to remember. Off to his right, just beyond the distorted faces and arms of his tribesmen, he saw his faithful pony and wondered why he was not riding the animal. He tried to speak, but his mouth felt like it was full of cotton. He swallowed hard, got the saliva flowing again.

"What happened?" asked the one who was called Turtle Belly.

"I do not know," Gray Wolf answered in his native tongue.

"Who did this to you?" asked another brave who was called Moccasins Too Big.

Again Gray Wolf had no answer. He started to sit up. Pain shot through the side of his head and forced him back down. He closed his eyes and tried to think. Parts of his dream flashed through his mind, but he couldn't bring them together. He brought his hand up, gently touched the place where the pain was so bad. The lump on the side of his head was the size of a hen's egg.

And then, with a sick, sinking feeling in his gut, he remembered everything.

"Plover Egg! And Little Killdeer," he said. "Are they here?"

Despite the pain that seared through his head when he moved, he sat up and quickly scanned the open meadow. In the distance, riding slowly toward them, he saw the six women of his tribe who had gone with the braves to take care of the bounty from the hunt. These women had cleaned the dead buffaloes, cut the meat up in big chunks, and wrapped them in the buffalo hides so they could be carried back to camp on a travois.

"What is it?" Moccasins Too Big asked. "What is it that troubles you? Are you hurt?"

"Where are the girls?" Gray Wolf demanded as he got to his feet. "They are gone!"

"We have just now come in from the hunt and found you here like this," Turtle Belly said. "We have not yet been to the camp, but Plover Egg and Little Killdeer will be there. They have no reason to be gone."

"No, they are gone," Gray Wolf insisted. "The white men came to our village and took Plover Egg and Little Killdeer away from us. I saw them, two white men, but I could not stop them. I could not risk hitting one of the girls with my arrows. One man hit me in the head with his rifle."

"How bad are you hurt?" Turtle Belly said, reaching out with both hands toward Gray Wolf's head.

"Not bad. I am good." When Turtle Belly's bronze arms stretched out toward him, another sleep-vision popped into Gray Wolf's head. He remembered the arms that tried to place Chief Yellow Dog's war bonnet on his head. He recalled how heavy the headdress had seemed to him in his dream and how he had tried to push it away.

"No, no! Chief Yellow Dog is dead!" he cried.

"How do you know this?" said Moon Bird, an older member of the tribe.

"I do not know for sure. I know it here, in my heart." Gray Wolf tapped his chest.

"The bump on your head makes you talk crazy," Turtle Belly said.

"No. These things are true," Gray Wolf protested. "I see the white men with my eyes."

"Do you know who they are?" Moccasins Too Big asked.

"The one who made this lump on my head calls himself Bolt. I tremble when I think of his evil look because I am afraid of what he will do to Plover Egg and Little Killdeer if we do not find them soon." Gray Wolf went to his pony and pulled himself up. "We must go to camp to see if Chief Yellow Dog still lives, and then we will prepare to track the men who stole our women. We must hurry, before it is too late."

The Indian braves mounted their ponies and followed Gray Wolf into the woods that stood between them and their temporary village.

When Gray Wolf rode out of the woods on the other side and saw the two squaws, Dancing Bear and Picks Many Berries, kneeling over the hide-covered mound on the ground, he knew that what he'd felt in his heart about Chief Yellow Dog was true.

"Chief Yellow Dog is dead. Yes?" Gray Wolf said as he rode into camp.

Dancing Bear looked up at her son. The flesh around her eyes was puffy and made her eyes seem even darker than they were. Her lips were drawn tight across her wide face, turned down at the corners.

"Yes, my son. Yellow Dog is dead. The white men come and kill our chief."

"They steal our daughters, too," sobbed Picks Many Berries.

"I know. We will find them." Gray Wolf dismounted and walked over to the place where the squaws squatted. He noticed Chief Yellow Dog's bow and buckskin quiver on the ground beside the chief's teepee. It saddened Gray Wolf to see it because the bow and quiver had hung idle on a peg in the chief's teepee for many moons, and Gray Wolf knew that his uncle had tried to defend the girls with his last breaths.

The chief's feathered war bonnet lay on the ground near the bow and quiver. Gray Wolf's heart grew heavier when he saw it and he knew why he'd tried to push it away in his dream. It wasn't the weight of the headdress itself that had bothered him, but the heavy sorrow in his heart for his uncle and the weight of the responsibilities that he would have to accept when the war bonnet became his.

Gray Wolf kneeled down beside his mother as the other braves gathered around. When he reached for the buffalo robe that covered Chief Yellow Dog's body, Picks Many Berries started to weep again. His heart hurt for her when he glanced over and saw the tears trickle down her dusty cheeks. Her lips moved as she began to mumble the low, guttural chants that proclaimed her sorrow for her dead husband. Her eyes were closed and she rocked gently back and forth in a trance.

Gray Wolf peeled the buffalo robe back slowly. Chief Yellow Dog looked peaceful in his eternal sleep. The wrinkles in his old, weathered face did not seem quite so deep or harsh as they had been when Gray Wolf last saw him on the morning he and the other braves had left for the buffalo hunt, just seven suns ago. The old chief's arms were folded across his bony chest the same way they usually were when he slept.

Gray Wolf saw no blood on his uncle's body, no bruises or wounds.

"How did he die?" he asked.

"The man with the evil eye shot him here." Dancing Bear raised Chief Yellow Dog's arm just enough for Gray Wolf to see the bullet hole in the chief's side.

Gray Wolf knew that the women had washed the blood away and made the chief look as good as possible. He leaned over and examined the wound, judged the size of the bullet that had killed Yellow Dog. He didn't need to roll the chief over and check his back to know that the bullet had torn a big chunk of flesh away when it exited the body.

His stomach knotted with anger, but he knew he had to let it go. Now, more than ever, he needed to think clearly. And, how many times had he heard his uncle say, "Accept in your heart as being true, those things which you have not the power to change." Well, Gray Wolf knew he didn't have the power to breathe life back into Chief Yellow Dog's old lungs. He had to concentrate now on finding Plover Egg and Little Killdeer.

After touching Yellow Dog's cold cheek briefly, he

pulled the buffalo robe back up and draped it over the chief's body, knowing that he would never see his uncle's face again. He was comforted only by the fact that he would carry Chief Yellow Dog's wisdom with him the rest of his life. He hugged his mother, offered his sympathy to Picks Many Berries, then stood up and faced the somber-faced men of his tribe.

"We must go quickly now and find Plover Egg and Little Killdeer," he told the men as he headed for his horse. "We must kill the man who has killed our chief and stolen our women."

"You are our chief now, Gray Wolf," Turtle Belly said as he reached out and placed his hand on his friend's shoulder. "We all know that is what Chief Yellow Dog wanted, and that is what we want, too."

"Yes, I am your chief now," Gray Wolf acknowledged before Turtle Belly took his hand away. "I will use Chief Yellow Dog's wisdom to guide us in all of the hard tasks that face us. We have to hurry now."

"We must have the ceremony to pass Chief Yellow Dog's war bonnet to you," the older brave named Moon Bird said. "We must sit and smoke Chief Yellow Dog's peace pipe before it passes to your hands for the rest of your days."

Another brave, Sits In Tall Grass, stepped forward. "First, we must bury Chief Yellow Dog and dance for our sorrow."

A warm breeze blew across Gray Wolf's chest, and yet the air was perfectly still at that moment. And then, Chief Yellow Dog's words came to him. "Always keep in your mind those things which are most important. Accomplish first the tasks which most need to be accomplished. If you do this, there will be time after that to do everything else that matters to you." In his mind, Gray Wolf could see his uncle sitting across from him on the cold night ground, the warm campfire burning between when everyone else had retired to their teepees. He could see Chief Yellow Dog staring down at the glowing embers as he shared with Gray Wolf his words of wisdom.

Gray Wolf glanced at each brave and knew it was time for him to take command.

"We must leave now to find the girls," he stated in a firm voice. "We have no time for the ceremonies now. We will have them when we return."

The youngest member of the tribe stepped over to Chief Yellow Dog's teepee and picked up the colorful headdress and held it up for everyone to see. "At least you will wear the chief's war bonnet?" asked Brave Bear, who had but fifteen years.

"No, Brave Bear," Gray Wolf said. "It is too unwieldy for me to wear while we track the white men."

"Shall we paint our faces and prepare for the war dance?" asked another young brave, Bites Mad Dog, who was two years older than Brave Bear.

"No, we must hurry. We do not even have time to unload the packs we carry on our ponies. Moon Bird, you stay here with the squaws," Gray Wolf said. "Sits In Tall Grass and Brave Bear, you stay, too. Prepare a burial ground for Chief Yellow Dog. The women of the hunt will be here soon with the buffalo meat and Moon Bird can perform the burial ceremony in my absence. The rest of you braves, mount your ponies and follow me."

"But, Gray Wolf, I should go with you to help find the girls," Brave Bear said. He set the chief's war bonnet down and ran toward Gray Wolf. "I have the keenest ear of all the braves and I shoot a straight arrow."

"I know," Gray Wolf said as he pulled himself up on his pony and took the reins in his hand. He looked down at Brave Bear and saw the disappointment on the young brave's face. Gray Wolf smiled for the first time since he had left his group of buffalo hunters at dawn that morning. "That is why I leave you here, Brave Bear. To protect the women. They will need your keen ear more than we."

With those words, Gray Wolf touched his moccasins to his pony's sides. The other braves followed him through the trees. Once he reached the meadow where he'd been attacked by the white men, he had no trouble following the path of trampled grass over to the far edge of the valley. He glanced up the slope and saw the fresh depressions in the ground where small rocks had been jarred loose. He guided his pony up the same trail to the road.

Once on the main road, he squinted his eyes and scanned the flat country in all directions. There was no sign of human life as far as he could see. He looked down at the hard ground and studied the hoof marks. He motioned for the braves to follow him and pointed to the north.

For a while, it was easy to follow the hoof prints in the dirt. About a mile up the road, he reached a place where the hoof prints became blurred in a pattern of confusion. Gray Wolf figured that the white men had stopped there and rested their horses, letting the animals mill around. He held an arm high in the air, signalling the braves to stop.

He jumped down from his pony and studied the ground more carefully.

"What is it?" Turtle Belly asked as he slid off his pony and joined his friend.

"There were more than two white men here," Gray Wolf said as the sick, sinking feeling came to his gut again. He pointed out the boot prints. "Big feet and little feet and look at the different patterns their boots make."

"Yes," agreed Turtle Belly. "There were as many as five men, maybe more. They were here long enough to smoke cigarettes. See the small butts."

Gray Wolf concentrated on a set of tracks made by a pair of large boots. He walked alongside the tracks and ended up at a cluster of oaks and cottonwoods. The trampled grasses and bent mesquite bushes led him a little farther. The sun, a big red ball low in the sky, blinded him for an instant. When he shaded his eyes and looked down into the meadow below, he was startled to see that from his vantage point, he had a clear view of his village. The teepees stood tall, stark against the backlighting of the sun. Even with his naked eyes, he could see his people moving about.

"This is where the bastards spied on our village before they raided it," he said with tight lips. "They knew the women were alone."

"Yes," said Turtle Belly, who had followed him there. "I see that one of them broke many twigs. He must have been nervous."

"They knew we were gone, dammit," said Gray Wolf. He saw that Turtle Belly was on his hands and knees, sniffing the ground.

"Yes. And one of the white eyes chews tobacco. See? This is where he spit it out."

Gray Wolf remembered something else that Chief Yellow Dog had told him: "When tracking someone, remember that every person has a habit, whether he knows it or not. Watch for the signs of it."

Gray Wolf turned and went back to his horse. "They make it easy for us to track them," he said.

"Yes, too easy. It might be a trick. We must be careful," warned Turtle Belly.

The braves rode north another mile or two before Gray Wolf stopped again. "The white men stopped here, too," he said as he slid off his pony.

He and Turtle Belly searched for new clues. Again they saw the remains of cigarettes, the broken twigs, but Gray Wolf saw something that made his heart jump. He stooped down and picked up a small piece of buckskin fringe.

"This came from one of the girls' dresses," he said sadly.

Turtle Belly examined it. "Maybe. Maybe not. It is hard to tell."

Gray Wolf kneeled down when he saw the wide, dark stain in the dirt. Thinking it was tobacco juice, he probed the earth with his finger, dug up a small bit of it, and smelled it. A chill went up his spine.

"This is blood," he said. "Is it from Plover Egg or Little Killdeer?"

"I don't know." Turtle Belly scrutinized the ground around the dark stain and found a small scrap of fabric that was stiff with dark-brown dried blood. "This is not buckskin," he said. "It is probably a piece of material from a man's shirt or trousers."

"I wounded one of the men with my tomahawk," Gray Wolf said. "I hit him in the leg and drew his blood."

"They must have stopped here to dress his wound. I smell something else." Turtle Belly crawled on his hands and knees for several feet, sniffing the ground like an anteater searching for his prey. "Yes, it is whiskey I smell. The white men were drinking whiskey. Enough whiskey was spilled on the ground for the odor to linger."

"We must hurry," Gray Wolf said as a sudden fear plunged into his heart. "We must find the girls before anything happens to them. We must kill the one who calls himself Bolt."

Chapter Eight

Bolt held Mary in his arms and felt her warmth seep through her robe. He had warmth of his own, deep in his loins, and wondered if she sensed it.

"Are you sure this is what you want?" he asked, his voice full of husk. He nuzzled his face against her soft, smooth neck while his hand roamed through her long, silky curls. Her hair smelled fresh and clean, her skin like a spring bouquet of lavenders. He felt her shiver and wished he knew what she was thinking.

He kissed a delicate place on her neck, traced a path up to her earlobe. His cock twitched and began to swell within his trousers.

She trembled again and then pulled away from him. When she looked up at him with her hungry eyes, he melted inside and had no more doubts.

"Yes, I want you, Bolt," she said, the husk in her voice matching his. "While you were gone, I wondered what it would be like to have you make love to me. When I thought about it, I imagined us going to bed together, our bodies touching for the first time. The sensation was so real, I could feel you entering me. It was so exciting, so good. Oh, Bolt, I hope you want to make love to me."

"I do," he whispered.

She took his arm and tugged him toward the bed. She faced him, worked the buttons of his chambray shirt until they were all undone. She pulled it open, then ran her fingers through his curly hairs.

Bolt threw her robe open. He looked down at her young, firm breasts for the first time. He touched them and felt her body tauten. The palms of his hands slid under the full breasts. He curled his fingers around the bare, velvet flesh and squeezed gently. She shuddered when he lowered his head and brushed his lips across first one nipple, then the other. He took a nipple into his mouth and heard her gasp. He teased it with his tongue until it hardened to a small rubbery nub.

"Ummmm," she sighed. "Nobody's ever done that to me before."

"You like it?" he mumbled as he switched to the other nipple.

"Yes, yes," she panted.

He unbuckled his gunbelt, lowered it to the floor next to the bed. He quickly undid the buttons of his trousers. He slid the pants down, kicked them to the side as he stepped out of them. He stood in front of her, his swollen shaft pressing against his shorts.

She threw her arms around his neck, tilted her chin up. She made a purring sound when his lips touched hers. Her tongue toyed at his lips, then slid into his mouth, sending a shock of electricity through him.

He pushed the robe off her shoulders, let his hands slide down her arms as the robe fell away and crumpled to the floor. He dropped his arms around her, moved his hands down to her bare buttocks, drew her close. Close enough so that he felt the contours of her body meld to his. Close enough so that he felt the warmth through his shorts when she thrust herself against his bulge.

He kissed her hard, felt her lips yield to his. Her

tongue quickly slithered into his mouth. It flicked back and forth across his own tongue with a wet, slippery promise of things to come.

Her hand slid inside his shorts, found his swollen manhood. She wrapped her fingers around the stalk, squeezed it. Fire shot through his loins. She pulled on it, then, still grasping it tightly, pushed her hand down to the base of his shaft, as if measuring it. As if not believing its size.

She broke the kiss, tilted her head back and stared up at him, her full lips parted sensually, her eyes glazed with desire.

"Oh, Bolt, you make me feel all funny inside. Weak and tingly. I—I feel all wet and slippery down there . . . between my legs."

Her words caused his cock to twitch in her hand. She squeezed it again, slid her hand up and down its length. She let go of it, tugged on his shorts, then dropped to the bed and scooted over to the middle.

Bolt looked down at her as he stripped out of his shorts. The late afternoon sun filtered through the curtain and bathed her in a golden glow. The shadows that fell across her accented her breasts, the mounds and valleys of her sensual body. He crawled in beside her, kissed each breast. He slid up to her face, kissed her lips with a burning passion.

His hand traveled down her body, slid over the mounds of each breast, across her flat, smooth belly, down to the nest of curly hairs. He caressed her gently between her legs, pressed on the soft folds of her sex. His finger traced a path across the slit of her pliant lips and he felt the hot dampness. God, he wanted her.

She gasped when he fingered her sheath. She reached down and grabbed his stiff shaft, tried to pull it toward her pussy. Her finger circled around the pulsing head of his cock, then slid over the slitted tip.

"You're wet, too," she said, as if surprised. She dabbed at the slippery juices that had leaked out of his slit, then smeared them around the swollen head with a delicate touch. She squeezed the shaft again, pumped her hand up and down.

Bolt could only moan, he wanted her so much. Did she know what she was doing to him with her probing fingers, her tugging hand?

"You're so . . . so big," she said.

"You made me that way," he said, his voice cracking with the husk of desire.

"Really?"

"Yes. You know how to make a man hot."

"Well, you've made me so hot I can hardly stand it. It feels so good every place you touch me."

"Good. It's supposed to." He kissed her passionately as he slid over on top of her so that his cock was buried between her legs, just inches from where he wanted it to be. He let his weight settle into her for a moment and felt her breasts crush against his chest. He spread her legs apart, kissed her again, then raised up above her.

He was so hot, he hesitated before he slid on up and touched the hot lips of her sex with the tip of his cock. Fire shot through his loins when he felt her damp heat between her legs.

She gasped when he touched her there, threw her head back on the pillow.

He pushed his cock gently against the damp slit. He felt her tense up.

"Will it fit?" She raised her head, stared down at his shaft. "You're so big."

"If you want me, it will."

"Yes, I want you now. Put it in me," she begged. She thrust her loins up at him.

He gripped her buttocks, drew her up to him as he

slid his cock inside the steaming, velvet lips of her sex. He felt the thin barrier of her maidenhead. Gently, he pushed a little harder, then pulled back.

"Do it," she cried. "Break it."

"I don't want to hurt you, Mary."

"I don't care. Do it fast."

He thrust his cock into her. Hard. Quick. He felt the barrier give under the pressure. She tensed for an instant, then surged into him as he plunged in deeper. He stroked her slowly at first and felt her rise up to meet him. He sank into her moist honeypot and felt her muscles tighten around him as he pulled his shaft back out. He pushed in again, deeper this time, and felt her pussy grip him like a vise, as if she were trying to keep him deep inside her.

The pace of their coupling was slow and even at first, like the constant washing of waves against a warm, sandy shore. He immersed himself in the golden pond of her wet pussy, bathed in the glow of her warmth, dipped into her again and again, always feeling the pulling, tugging, clutching of her sex. Always smelling the sweet dankness of her special musk.

He slid his hand out from under her buttocks, brought it up to her breast. He caressed the smooth, pliable mound, suckled at her nipple like a ravenous baby. And all the while, he heard her murmur soft utterances in his ear, mumbled expressions of her wild passion that he could not understand.

He continued to plunge his cock into her hot, gripping sheath and, without missing stroke, he moved his lips up to her full, sensual mouth. She purred and cooed when he covered her lips with his hungry mouth. He pushed his tongue inside where it was as warm and wet as she was between her legs. He flicked his tongue against hers with the same rhythm that he used to plumb her depths with his rigid stalk.

He broke the kiss, finally, and moved his head over and nuzzled it against her cheek where he smelled the lavender scent of her soap, the heady fragrance of the perfume she'd dabbed behind her ears. He pushed down on her shoulders, stroked her faster, deeper, as his passion mounted.

Mary became a squirming wild animal under him, her hips undulating, bucking as she matched his rhythm with her own passion. She grunted and squealed and made noises like a rooting pig. And when Bolt thought he would explode his seed, he heard her moan, felt her body shudder as the waves of orgasm flooded over her.

"Stop," she cried.

With his cock buried deep inside her, Bold paused, lifted his head and looked down at her.

"Did I hurt you?"

"No, no. It's so good, so good," she cried as she squirmed beneath him. Her hips started bucking up and down as she begged for more.

Bolt plunged into her with a new fury. He sank his shaft deep into her steaming cauldron, thrust it in and out of her. Flesh slapped against bare flesh as he plowed into her furrow again and again. She matched each stroke with one of her own, pausing only briefly when the orgasms came. He bored into her, mindless of her fingers digging into his flesh.

He plunged his cock clear to the hilt as his own orgasm came and jolted him with a rocking, throbbing ecstasy. He collapsed, and when he'd caught his breath, rolled off her, totally spent.

Bolt drew in a deep breath and relaxed, contented to feel the warmth of Mary's bare flesh against his. His racing heartbeat began to slow as he closed his eyes and smelled the scent of their twin musks as it drifted up to his nostrils. Finally, he began to cool off as the sweat evaporated from his body. He felt no pressure, no need to hurry off, a feeling that was rare for him.

"Bolt?" Mary said a short while later.

"Yeah?"

"What's it like to be a harlot?" she asked as she stared up at the ceiling.

"I reckon I wouldn't know much about that," he laughed. He glanced over at her and saw the look of contentment on her radiant face when she turned her head toward him and smiled. He knew it was all in his imagination, but he thought she looked more mature, more like a woman now. Maybe it was true that sex changed a woman.

"Yes, you do. I want to know," she persisted.

"Why? You're not still thinking about—thinking about becoming a harlot, are you?"

"Well, I'm not a virgin anymore," she said smugly, pretending to be haughty about the whole thing.

Bolt felt a pang of jealousy, which surprised him because he didn't get jealous. He believed in living his life the way he wanted to, as long as he didn't hurt anyone intentionally, and in letting other people live their lives. He just didn't want to think about it so soon after he'd made love to her.

"You wouldn't like it," he grumbled.

"I might," she teased, snuggling her bare body over next to his.

"Just remember, I don't sleep with the harlots who work for me."

Mary's infectious laughter surprised him. It sounded like the tinkling music of a dozen small bells, each one rung a split second after the other, until they all reverberated together.

"Well, I guess that kills any ideas about working for you," she smiled. She stretched her hand out and squeezed his arm. "Oh, Bolt, you made me feel so

88

good, I don't ever want to sleep with anyone else, but, I'm still curious about that kind of life. If sex feels so good, why is being a harlot so bad?"

"It isn't bad. A lot of folks think there's something evil or dirty about it, but prostitutes provide a necessary service and the prostitutes I know are more ladylike than the ladies who complain about them. But being a harlot isn't an easy lot."

"It seems like it'd be easy, especially if you knew you were making some man happy." Mary turned toward Bold and propped herself up on her elbow. She ran her fingers through his hair, stroked his forehead. "Did I make you happy, Bolt?"

"Yes. That's what made it so special." He lifted his head, kissed her tenderly, basked in her affectionate attention.

"I thought all a harlot had to do was make a man happy, but it's more than that, isn't it?"

"That's part of it, but like I told you before, most whores don't like men and they don't enjoy sex. Yes, they have to satisfy the men, but they just do it for the money—and I don't think that's what you need. The main problem is that when a girl becomes a prostitute, she doesn't get to choose her partner. He chooses her."

"What you mean is that a harlot has to sleep with any man who has the money to pay for her time, whether he's dirty or drunk, or just plain mean."

Bolt saw her shudder.

"In most whorehouses that's true, but not in my place. If a fellow's slobbering drunk when he comes in, we kick him out. I've seen too many girls mistreated."

"Why would a fellow hurt a girl if he wanted to have sex with her?" Mary tilted her head, gave Bolt a puzzled look.

"Who knows what makes people tick?" Some men are all twisted inside and they take it out on the prostitutes, or any other gal they meet up with."

"I'm glad you're not that way, Bolt." She lowered her head, kissed his eyelids, then gave him a brief, tender kiss on his lips.

"I think every woman should be treated with respect, no matter what she does. That's why we protect our gals as much as we can and we don't make them sleep with a fellow if they don't want to."

"Really? I'd think you'd lose customers that way, and money."

"Money isn't important, and the kind of customers we'd lose aren't the kind of fellows we'd want around the bordello anyway. I figure if a gal isn't happy, she isn't gonna make the customers happy. So we pay the girls a decent salary and make the working conditions as pleasant as possible."

"You know, Bolt, I'd like to see your ranch and meet your girls. Do you suppose I could ride out there with you?"

"I don't know why not. I think the girls would like to meet you, too, and we've got a couple of spare cottages where you could stay. We'll ride out after supper and you can stay with us until you're ready to go back to Fort Worth."

Mary smiled down at him and stroked his cheek. He snatched her hand and peppered it with kisses.

"You know, Aunt Millie was right about you, Bolt. You're a mighty decent fellow."

"I've been called worse," he grinned.

She leaned down and kissed him, and he felt her bare breasts press into his chest. Her hand moved slowly down his belly, toward his crotch. Goosebumps popped out on his flesh as her fingertips just barely brushed across his sensitive skin. She took his limp mass in her hand, began to knead it to life.

"You do that and you'll make it hard again."

"I wouldn't mind that," she cooed, her voice low and throaty. "After supper, maybe we could come back up here for a little while before we go out to your ranch. I mean, why waste the room? After all, you paid good money for it."

"You're a hussy, Mary," he grinned.

Relaxed and completely contented, Bolt let his head sink into the pillow and closed his eyes. He felt very comfortable with Mary beside him, and at the moment, he didn't have a worry in the world.

Chapter Nine

Jack Ramsey stood back and watched his men scoop out a shallow grave with their tin cups. The constant scraping and clinking of metal against rock was making him edgy and the wad of tobacco in his mouth did little to calm his nerves.

The sun looked like a big orange ball sinking slowly to meet the horizon as it dipped low in the western sky. Ramsey stood just beyond the fence lines of the southwest back forty of Bolt's ranch property. All around him, long shadows stretched out from the trees and bushes and crawled across the uneven landscape. The deep riverbed, which ran along the south edge of Bolt's property, was already covered by evening shadow. Way off in the distance, beyond several rolling hills, sunlight glinted off the windows of Bolt's ranch house and the sprawling bordello on the hill below the house.

Hatred boiled up in Ramsey as he stared briefly at the distant whorehouse with its six separate cottages out back. He couldn't forget the night he'd gone there and, by chance, had seen his sister leading some slimy ruffian out the back door toward one of the cottages. Emblazoned in his mind forever was the image of

Linda in her brief, bright red, seductive garment as she walked out that back door, draping herself all over the dirty son of a bitch while the slobbering bastard kissed her and pawed at her breasts and played with her pussy with his filthy hands.

He remembered every little detail as if he could see it right then. He remembered how Linda's breasts spilled over the top of her outfit and how the short red skirt just barely covered her pussy and buttocks. He remembered how much of her legs were exposed, even though they were covered by those black net stockings. He recalled how she smiled up at the man, tempting him with her puckered red lips, her open mouth. And how she wiggled her hips and thrust her pussy at him, inviting him to touch her there.

Suddenly, Ramsey couldn't stand to think about it anymore. He spit a stream of tobacco juice to the ground and turned away, his heart hardening to solid rock. Soon enough he would get his revenge from Bolt for turning his sister into a goddamn whore who had to spread her legs for every drooling bastard who came along.

Hutch road up and stopped beside Ramsey. He slid from his horse, took his hat off, wiped his brow with his shirt-sleeve, then slid the hat back in place.

"Ain't no injuns in sight," he said. "Big Mac and I rode clear up to the top of the slope on the other side of the river where we could see forever. There just ain't no injuns out there."

"They'll come," Ramsey said. "And when they do, you and I'll be watching from that hill over there."

Hutch turned and saw the clump of trees Ramsey was pointing at.

"What about the others?" he asked. Aren't they gonna be here?"

"No, I don't want a bunch of horses standin' around

when the injuns show up. I told the men that as soon as they were through here, they could ride on into town and make a night of it."

"Don't look like Oppie needs no more to drink." Hutch shook his head. "The way he's been drinkin' in this heat today, I'm surprised he's still on his feet."

"That's his problem. As long as he don't mess up my plans, he can drink the whole damned town dry when he gets there."

Ramsey knew time was running short and wondered how much longer it would take his men to finish the excavation. In a half-hour the sun would disappear, and then they'd have only another thirty minutes or so of dusk light before it turned dark. He didn't need the light for himself or his men, but he wanted the Comanches who would track them to find the grave before dark.

So far, his plan was going like clockwork. He just didn't want to run into any snags now when they were so close to setting everything in place.

He cursed the ground that was dry and hard and full of big rocks. The four men had been on their knees, digging, for nearly an hour, pausing occasionally just long enough to wipe the sweat from their brows before it trickled down into their eyes. The wide, six-by-eight-foot hole was almost four inches deep and Ramsey didn't want it much deeper.

He glanced over at the limp, lifeless bodies of the two Indian maidens and felt no remorse, no guilt. The small bodies, bruised and dirt-stained from being raped on the hard earth, were sprawled out on the ground a few yards from the grave, mute testimonies to the shame and brutality they had been forced to endure. Their slender arms and legs were still in the same awkward positions as they were when the girls had collapsed to the ground after they'd been choked to death.

Their dirty, dusty buckskin dresses, now stained with dried semen, had been ripped open all the way down the front by the vicious slashes of Hutchinson's knife before the men had taken their turns with the girls. Those dresses lay open now and Ramsey stared at the bronze bodies that he had thought so sensual before. He saw their small breasts that the men had fondled so roughly, their flat tummies, their private places between their legs where the men had taken turns raping them.

Pesky flies buzzed the bare flesh, settled on the raw bruises on the girls' faces where the men had slapped them when they protested with every bit of strength they had. Other flies swarmed and gathered at the girls' crotches, which had been bloodied by the vicious attacks of the outlaws.

Ramsey hadn't taken his turn at the girls. Neither had Oppie Shenker. Oppie had been drinking all afternoon and when the time came, he had tried like hell to jam his limp prick into one of the Indian maidens, but he was too drunk to get an erection. That was when Ramsey had gotten the first inkling that there was dissension among his men. The hard outlaws had made fun of Oppie, ragged his ass for not being man enough to rape a helpless Indian girl. Ramsey had seen the flare of hatred in Oppie's eyes before Oppie had gone off to sulk and suck on his flask.

Ramsey's leg had hurt too much for him to participate in the mass rape, but he didn't care about that part of it anyway. Not any more. Not like he had when he'd first seen the Indian maidens through his binoculars. He was more concerned with getting the girls buried near Bolt's ranch, in a grave shallow enough for the Indians to find it and dig it up, than he was in sex. His obsession with getting his revenge from Bolt had consumed his mind and taken away his sex drive.

On Ramsey's orders, Kyle Hutchinson and Vernon Tate had done the actual killing by choking the girls to death. Hutch had suggested shooting the girls in the head, but Ramsey didn't want the guns fired. He didn't want any of Bolt's ranch hands snooping around. Not only that, Ramsey didn't know if the Comanches were on their trail yet and he sure as hell didn't want them showing up while they were burying the girls.

For a time, Ramsey had considered slitting the girls' throats from ear to ear, just to further infuriate the Indians. But as he looked at the caked blood between the girls' legs, he knew that the Indians would realize that their maidens had been treated brutally.

Ramsey looked at the sun again. "That's deep enough," he told his men. "Just stick the girls in the ground and cover them up."

Hutch and Fess Grodin carried Little Killdeer's body to the shallow grave and set it down, straightened her arms and legs. Big Mac Sloan scooped Plover Egg's limp body up in both arms, and placed it beside the other one.

"This hole ain't deep enough." Oppie stared up at Ramsey with bleary eyes. He was still on his knees beside the grave where he'd done less than his share of the digging.

"Yes it is," Ramsey said. "I want that grave to stick up high enough for them damned injuns to trip over it. But don't pile too much dirt on top. I want to make it easy for 'em to dig it up."

"Shame we had to kill 'em," Big Mac said as he started to scoop dirt into the grave with his foot. "They was kinda purty before we slapped 'em around."

"Yeah," agreed Fess Grodin as he kneeled down and shoved a pile of dirt into the hole with both hands. "Especially Little Killdeer. I hated like hell to hit her but she fought me like a wild tiger. Look here where she scratched me."

"Hell, them gals is all used up," Oppie slurred in his slow southern drawl. "Nobody'd want 'em now. Not even their own kin."

"Just keep jawin' if you want to be here when the injuns show up, Oppie," Tate said. "The rest of us are going to town for a little funnin'."

"Hell, I'm goin' with ya," Oppie said. "I'm gonna get a little pussy tonight."

"Shit, in your condition, you couldn't get it up if some gal sucked on it for an hour," Tate taunted.

"Hell, you're just a kid, Tate. What would you know about women?" Oppie said. He swayed as he looked up at Vernon with an idiotic grin on his face. "I'll bet you was still a virgin until you stuck your dinky prick in that injun gal today."

Ramsey saw Tate's eyes flash with anger. For a minute he thought there would be a scuffle, but he didn't interfere. He believed that the men should handle their own squabbles.

Tate glanced around at the other men. None of them were paying any attention to him or Oppie. They were busy dumping dirt over the bodies.

"If you wasn't so drunk, I'd knock your head off." He moved around to the other side of the grave, grabbed up his tin cup. His teeth clenched with anger, he scooped up a cup of dirt and tossed it in the hole.

Ramsey stood above the grave and watched the flies swarm around as the dirt and rocks gradually filled in the hole and covered the lifeless bodies.

"That's enough dirt," he said. "Just pile a few rocks in the middle so they won't miss it."

A few minutes later, after rocks and stones had been tossed onto the grave, Big Mac Sloan asked if they were done.

"Yeah," said Ramsey. "You fellows go on into town and have a good time for yourselves. Hutch and I are gonna wait around here for a while and see what happens. Most likely, we'll ride in later to celebrate with you, but either way, we'll see you in the morning."

Ramsey leaned down, scooped up a handful of dirt with both hands. He felt cold inside, and hard as a slab of granite, as he let the dirt filter through his fingers to cover the only part of Plover Egg's face that was still visible. Covering Plover Egg's face was a small thing to do, and yet, that small gesture of finality swelled him with a keen sense of fulfillment. It was as if he'd finally buried that ugly, intolerable part of his sister that he'd grown to hate so much.

Ramsey brushed the dirt from his hands and limped away from the shallow grave. He'd done all he could do and he was immensely satisfied. He'd made his move in this game of revenge. Now it was up to someone else to make the next move.

Gray Wolf and his braves had no trouble following the trail. The white men who had killed Chief Yellow Dog and stolen their women had made no effort to cover their tracks. Gray Wolf figured that the white men were either too dumb to think that the Comanches would follow them, or they just didn't give a damn . . .

"The white men head for San Antonio," said Turtle Belly when they stopped at the river to check for sign.

"Yes. San Antonio is a big village. That must be where Bolt has his whorehouse," said Gray Wolf. He held his hand up, lined the bottom edge of his palm up with the horizon. He squinted against the glare of the bright sun, measured the distance between the sun and the horizon. "One finger," he announced. "The sun will go to sleep soon. We must hurry."

Gray Wolf squatted down at the edge of the shallow river that he and his men had just crossed. He dipped his hand into the cool water, brought it up and drank from his hand.

Turtle Belly stood beside him. "Do you think Plover Egg and Little Killdeer are safe?" the short, heavyset Indian asked in a solemn voice.

"I do not know that," sighed Gray Wolf as he stared down into the clear water. "There was something in my sleep-thoughts that makes me afraid, but I cannot bring it to my mind."

"But you are so brave, Gray Wolf. I did not think you ever knew fear."

"Yes. Whenever I think of my sister and Little Killdeer in the hand of those dirty, ugly men, I can feel my heart beat fast. I can feel the butterflies dance in my stomach. Chief Yellow Dog felt these things many times, he told me, when a member of his tribe was in danger. Like Yellow Dog, I do not fear for my own life, for only for our women."

"We must avenge Chief Yellow Dog's death."

"Yes," said Gray Wolf as he stood up, "but first we must find Plover Egg and Little Killdeer."

Gray Wolf mounted his pony and led the other braves up the slope of the riverbank. Once they were on flat land again, they spread out so that each brave could watch the ground. Turtle Belly rode alongside Gray Wolf. They had not ridden far when the sun disappeared, taking with it the long shadows from the ground.

Gray Wolf checked the western sky more than once as he rode. The white puffs of clouds took on a pink hue, then gradually turned to purple.

"We ride slower now so that we do not lose sight of the tracks," Gray Wolf said when the grayness of evening began to settle over the flat countryside. Off in the distance he saw the orange glow of lamplight that spilled from the windows of a few shadowy structures. For a minute, he thought they might be nearing San Antonio, but quickly realized that there were not enough buildings to make up a town the size of San Antonio.

As the earth gave up the last bits of its color to the gray cloak of dusk, the braves continued to follow the tracks made by the horses of the white men.

"They stopped here," Gray Wolf said when the hoofprints became cluttered and confusing. It was almost dark and he had to strain his eyes to see the ground.

The braves reined up and dismounted, as they had done each time they'd come across a place where the white men had stopped before them. Hunched over like doddering old men, they began to scrutinize the ground. For a few minutes, the only sound in the hushed evening air was that of moccasins shuffling across the hard earth.

"They were here not long ago," called Red Feather.

"What is it?" Gray Wolf said as he and the others ran toward Red Feather.

"This wad of tobacco. It is still wet." Red Feather held the small wad up for the others to feel.

"Then we are not far behind them," said Crooked Arrow. "We can ride faster than the white men."

"The darkness will slow us down," said Gray Wolf. "It will not be easy to follow their tracks."

Red Feather kicked at something dark on the ground, then stooped to pick it up. "Here is more tobacco," he said. "They stayed her longer than they did at the other places where they stopped."

"Then we must search this ground with more care before we leave," Gray Wolf said. He glanced over at the western sky and saw that the drifting purple clouds had turned a leaden gray. A feeling of desperation settled over him. He knew that when they left this place, they would lose the white men's tracks in the darkness. It would be the night of the full moon, but that light wouldn't come for a little while.

The braves went back to searching for anything that would give them a fresh clue about the girls and the men who had stolen them.

Gray Wolf was the one who spotted the small mount of dirt. He almost missed it, but when the ground seemed to take on a different texture under his moccasins, he sensed that something was wrong. He took several steps and felt the loose rocks under his sensitive feet. He scanned the dark land around him, and then he spotted it, way off to his right. When he saw the low, dark mound that rose out of the ground, his stomach was suddenly full of roiling bear grease.

As he ran over to the mound, that part of his sleep-thoughts that he hadn't been able to recall before, came rushing back to him. He knew in his heart what he would find under the pile of dirt.

He dropped to the ground and clawed at the loose dirt with his bare hands.

"Over here!" he called. "I have found something."

The other braves dashed over and scooped the dirt from the pile.

Gray Wolf felt something under his hands. He stopped digging and quickly brushed the dirt away from the flesh. Suddenly, in the lingering gray light of the day, he found himself staring down at the badly bruised face of his sister. The overpowering pain of grief welled up in his chest, stabbed at his fluttering heart. He bit his lip, batted back the tears that sprung to his eyes.

Gray Wolf could do nothing but stare at Plover Egg's battered face. They had come so close to finding the girls while there was still a chance for them to live. He thought about the rest of his small tribe and knew the sorrow his mother and Picks Many Berries would feel in their hearts when they learned that they had lost their only daughters to the white men.

Chief Yellow Dog's words came to him then, as they always did when he needed them: "Accept in your heart as being true, those things which you have not the power to change." Gray Wolf had to accept the death of Plover Egg and Little Killdeer as being true. As brave and mighty as he might be, he had not the power to bring them back to this life.

The others continued to scrape the dirt away from the limp bodies and Gray Wolf was stunned to see the torn dresses, the bare flesh of their bodies, the dark stains between their legs. He thought about the cruelty of the men who had raped the girls. He thought about the horror the girls must have gone through during their last minutes of life.

As he stared down at Plover Egg's face, he made a silent promise to her. He vowed to avenger her death, and Little Killdeer's, just as he would avenge Chief Yellow Dog's death. An eye for an eye. He wouldn't stop until he had killed every last one of those murdering, raping, white bastards.

And then, for a brief moment, he closed his eyes and let the quiet sobs come.

On a dark, distant hill, hidden by the trees, Jack Ramsey watched the Indians and gloated.

Chapter Ten

Gray Wolf's heart was heavy with grief as the darkness of night blotted out the surrounding landscape. It seemed like the only shreds of dim, gray light remaining in the evening sky lingered over the cluster of sad Indian braves who huddled around the shallow grave.

The stench of cow piles hung heavy in the evening air; Gray Wolf couldn't smell the mustiness of the white man's sweat that he had sniffed before.

He leaned closer and glanced at the battered faces of Plover Egg and Little Killdeer, glad that the darkness had finally obscured the hideousness of their tortured, naked bodies. In the dim light, his sister's face seemed even more distorted from the swollen bruise around her eye and the dirt-covered cuts on her cheeks and chin than it had a few minutes before, in the glow of dusk.

He gently placed his hand on Plover Egg's cheek and was startled by the lack of warmth to her flesh, even though he'd accepted the fact that she was dead. A chill crept up his spine and he didn't know if it was caused by an evening breeze or by the fact the he hadn't thought about his sister's body turning cold and stiff.

Gray Wolf withdrew his hand quickly, rose from the

ground, stretched up to his full height. His arms rippled with sinew as he folded them across his strong, muscled chest. He stood erect, his neck stiff, his chin tucked back, the skin stretched tight across his high, wide cheekbones. His heart swelled with a feeling of power as he stared straight ahead.

"Our people are proud. We will not allow this atrocity to our women to go unnoticed," he said with fierce determination, his calm voice tinged with the hatred he held in his heart for the white men. "We will avenge these brutal murders of our precious sisters, Plover Egg and Little Killdeer. Just as we will avenge the death of our brave chief who died for these girls."

The braves stood up and quietly raised their hands above their heads in agreement.

Gray Wolf stepped back away from the grave. The other braves lowered their arms and gathered around him in a close circle.

"Crooked Arrow and Moccasins Too Big," Gray Wolf addressed the two men closest to him, "—You will wrap the bodies in your extra blankets and prepare them for the sad journey back to our people."

"Shall we return to our village when we have wrapped the bodies?" Red Feather asked.

"Yes. You will have a slow trip in the dark. We will catch up with you along the way."

"Where will you go, our chief?" asked Moccasins Too Big.

"To save time, we will go to the nearby ranch," he said. He extended his arm straight out and pointed to the flickering orange glows in the distance. "We will ask the people there if they know a man called Bolt. They might know the location of his bordello."

Walking Stick stepped forward. Now that Chief Yellow Dog was dead, Walking Stick was the oldest member of the tribe.

"Gray Wolf," he said, "I am just now remembering something that might help you."

"What is it?"

"Do you remember when Chief Yellow Dog sent me to find his friend, Chief Running Fox, at the Comanche village north of San Antonio? It was many moons ago, when the streams ran dry."

"Yes, that is when the illness first came to Yellow Dog."

"That was when my pony turned lame and I had to kill him."

"I remember."

"When I found myself in need of another pony to carry me north, I stopped at that very ranch house." Walking Stick nodded toward the distant structure. "I know it is the same because of the river that flows nearby. I planned to pay for the horse, but nobody was home. Because my need was great, I took a horse from the stable, then stopped at a white man's saloon, hoping to find the animal's owner."

"That was a dangerous thing to do," said young Bites Mad Dog.

"Yes, but I had no desire to steal from the white man. He had not harmed me and I did not wish to harm him," Walking Stick said in rapid, guttural words. "The white men were hostile to me. They called me a horse thief and threatened me with big guns. But before they chased me away, an old man told me that the ranch and the horses in the stable belonged to a man who had just died, a man called King. The old man said that a stranger had bought the ranch that very day, with plans to turn it into a bordello."

"Did you learn the name of the stranger who bought the ranch?" Gray Wolf asked.

"No. With the big guns pointed at me, I did not stay there long. But I think it may be this Bolt you are looking for."

"If you are right, this task we face will not take long. We will go there with caution."

Gray Wolf glanced down at the grave one last time and was sad, but relieved, that he could not see his sister's face in the dark. He wanted to remember her the way she was when she smiled and laughed, when her face was bright with joy, as if she'd been given a chunk of the sun.

Like silent, stalking animals in the night, Gray Wolf and four of his braves rode across the fields.

A horse whinnied from somewhere across the dark land and the sound jarred Gray Wolf's senses.

"What was that?" whispered Bites Mad Dog, the youngest brave who was with them.

"A horse," said Gray Wolf. He looked in that direction but couldn't see anything except the dim contours of the rolling hills and an occasional clump of trees. In the darkness, the clusters of trees took on odd, ominous shapes that gave him an eerie feeling. A man, or a group of men, could easily use the trees for cover.

He sniffed the night air and still, he could smell nothing but the cow dung.

He didn't like it. All along, he'd had a strange feeling that he and his braves were walking into a trap. The trail had been too easy to follow. Even the shallow grave had not been concealed. It was almost as if someone wanted them to stumble over it.

From another direction, an owl screeched a warning.

Gray Wolf's head whirled around.

A cow bellowed. Then another.

"Cattle," Gray Wolf said without being asked. "This is a cattle ranch. You can smell the foul stench of their droppings."

"Yes," said Bites Mad Dog. "Do you think they would have pleasure girls on a ranch?"

"I don't know. I see light from more than one structure. Perhaps one of them is the ranch house and another the house of pleasure."

Another sound came to Gray Wolf's ears, this time so low and muffled that he just barely detected it with his keen hearing. He reined up, held up his hand. The other braves pulled up and stopped around him.

"What is it?" Bites Mad Dog whispered.

"Quiet." He cocked his head, strained his ear. "Yes, it is music I hear. . . . a piano. And something else. Laughter and the voices of young women."

"Your young ears are much better than mine," said Walking Stick.

Gray Wolf gave the signal for them to continue.

"Be careful," he warned his men. "Use the eyes in the back of your head to see behind you."

"What do you mean?" asked Bites Mad Dog.

"You will make a good warrior some day, Bites Mad Dog," Gray Wolf laughed. "You are inquisitive, like I was when I was Chief Yellow Dog's pupil."

He smiled and remembered the first time Chief Yellow Dog had said that to him. Gray Wolf had had but ten years at the time and he was puzzled by Yellow Dog's strange words. When Yellow Dog had seen Gray Wolf reach back and examine his head for the extra eyes, the chief had laughed and told him that he meant for the boy to use all of his senses when there was a chance that he might be in danger.

"You are the teacher now," said Bites Mad Dog.

Gray Wolf thought about it and realized that it was his responsibility to pass on to the others those truths that Yellow Dog had taught him.

As they rode closer to the first dwelling that spilled light from its window, the music stopped. And when it did, the sounds of laughter and happy young voices grew louder. He spotted the two horses tied to a hitchrail near the log building. Even in the dim light from the windows, he knew that the horses were not the ones the two white men had ridden when they raided the Indian village.

He saw the silhouettes of six small cottages behind the large, two-story log cabin. Lamplight filtered through heavy curtains at the windows of four of them. The cottages on each end of the row were dark. Hurricane lamps, hanging from posts, lit a path between the cottages and the bigger buildings.

Gray Wolf stopped a hundred yards from the bordello. He slid down from his pony.

"This must be the bordello," he said, "and the big house up there on the hill must be the home where Bolt lives."

"I think you are right," said Walking Stick. "When I was here before, I went to the big house on the hill to inquire about a horse. When I went to the stable, I saw this dwelling here, but I don't remember seeing any small cottages."

"Then he has added them. It is time to avenge the death of our loved ones. We are going to take two of Bolt's girls. We will take them far away from here." Gray Wolf's voice became cold and even, sharp as a stiletto, when he spoke. "We will rape them, and murder them, and bury their sullied bodies in shallow graves for the animals to feed on, just as Bolt and his friends have done to our Plover Egg and Little Killdeer."

"Yes," said Walking Stick. "This is what we must do. An eye for an eye. That is what Chief Yellow Dog has taught us."

"Turtle Belly, you come with me. I want to check out this building and see if Bolt and his friends are here before we steal his women. Walk softly. We must be careful."

Gray Wolf and Turtle Belly left their ponies with the other braves and made their way up to the bordello. The plinking notes of the piano floated out on the air just as the two braves reached the front of the building.

Gray Wolf noticed that the windows were open and the door was propped open with a small keg to take the day's heat away. He ducked down and snuck over to a large window, motioned Turtle Belly to follow him. He stuck his head up just high enough to peek inside.

He saw right away that there were two men in the living room, and five pretty, young girls who wore tight-fitting, low-cut frocks and too much powder and rouge on their faces. The room was massive, with two large sofas and several overstuffed chairs, a braided rug between the two sofas.

Gray Wolf studied the face of the man who sat on one of the sofas with a pretty blond girl snuggled up beside him. He knew the man was not one of the white eyes who had come to his village.

He could not see the face of the other man who stood with another of the girls at the bar across the room. Next to the bar, with its sparkling crystal glasses and bottles of whiskey, a girl with blond hair plunked the keys of the piano. The two girls who were not busy with the men sat in comfortable chairs and talked to the girl at the piano.

"Are those the men who attacked our village?" Turtle Belly whispered.

"No," Gray Wolf said when he saw the man at the bar turn to speak to the one who played the piano. "They are not the ones we are looking for. Hush. Listen to what they say."

"Where's Bolt tonight, Harmony?" the handsome lawyer at the bar said to the piano player. He wore a neat brown business suit and still smelled of aftershave lotion from his trip to the barber just before he had ridden out to Bolt's bordello at the Rocking Bar Ranch.

"I don't know, George. I thought he'd be back in time for supper. He and Tom left early this morning to pick up the new girl who came in on the two o'clock stage. Tom got back just as we were sitting down to supper, but I don't know what happened to Bolt and the girl."

The timing was right, thought Gray Wolf. If Bolt and his friend left early that morning, they would have had time to ride out to the Comanche village and be back by now. He wondered where Bolt had gone now and why he hadn't returned with his friend. Probably had gone to town to celebrate, the cold-hearted bastard.

"I wouldn't worry about it, Harmony."

"Oh, I don't worry about Bolt," she laughed. "He's a big boy and he can take care of himself. And from what Tom says, the new girl is big enough to take care of the both of them."

"Well, when you see Bolt, tell him I can get those fifty head of cattle he wanted."

"Tom's up at the house if you want to talk to him," Harmony said.

"Not tonight. Not when I can be with this pretty little gal." The man called George squeezed the dark-haired girl beside him.

Gray Wolf had seen all he needed to see, heard all he needed to hear. He snuck away from the window, with Turtle Belly right behind him, and picked his way back into the darkness, where the other braves waited for them.

Off to the east, the moon pushed its way out of the ground and threw a silver cast across the earth.

"Bolt isn't here at the ranch," Gray Wolf told his men. "We will steal the two girls now and seek our revenge with Bolt and his men later."

"Will we all go with you to get the girls?" asked Bites

Mad Dog.

"Yes, we will surprise them with our numbers. I want to dash in there, snatch up the girls, and be out of there with the speed of a swift arrow. Ground-tie the ponies and get ready to go. Bring your bows and tomahawks."

The piano music started up again as the braves followed Gray Wolf up to the bordello. He stopped a few feet away from the open door, spoke in a loud whisper. His men had to strain to hear his voice above the din that floated out through the doorway.

"We will take the girls who sit by themselves in big chairs," Gray Wolf instructed. "Walk on soft moccasins. They will be so surprised, they will not know we are in there until we are already gone. Go in with your tomahawks in hand, but remember, this is not a massacre. We want only two of their women and we want to take them alive."

"Yes," said Turtle Belly. "We are with you."

"We must be quick," Gray Wolf added. "We must steal the girls before Bolt's friend can come down from the big house on the hill. Are you ready to attack?"

Each brave held his tomahawk up in a silent reply.

The Comanche braves snuck up to the doorway. When Gray Wolf gave the signal, they moved into the room quickly, their tomahawks ready. They froze, assumed a stance that looked like they were ready to pounce. Nobody saw them come in. They paused long enough for each man to get his bearings.

The couple who had been on the plush soft when Gray Wolf had peered in the window were still there. The man and the soiled dove were talking, their lips almost touching, backs to the door. The girl who placed the piano also had her back to the door.

Gray Wolf saw that the man and the young, painted hussy who had been at the bar now strolled through a

111

dim hallway that led to the back door.

He was glad to see that the two girls that he wanted to steal were still in their chairs, singing the words to the piano tune. He could see only the head of the one girl who sat with her back to him. Her red curly hair stuck up above the back of her overstuffed chair. The girl with the blond hair sat with her feet tucked up under her, her head turned toward the piano.

The two buxom girls were happy, carefree, as they sang along with the music.

As far as Gray Wolf was concerned, neither one of them would ever smile again.

Gray Wolf glanced at each of his men. Each nodded his readiness.

"Dammit, I wish I knew what was going on," Jack Ramsey cursed from a dark, distant hill as he sat his horse. He spit a long stream of tobacco juice to the ground.

"You want a shot of whiskey?" asked Hutch. He snagged the flask from his waistband, handed it to his friend.

Ramsey took it, tipped his head back and took a long drag, then gave the flask back.

Hutch drank from the container before he tucked it away. "Look at that moon coming up over there," he said. "It's gonna be a full one tonight. Ought to make them injuns good and crazy."

"Yeah," Ramsey mumbled as he stared in the direction of the bordello. "I can't hear nothin' but them damned bawlin' cows. We can't even see the bordello from here."

"Do you want to ride closer?" Hutch asked.

"Hell, no. That damned horse of yours almost gave us away. Did you see them injuns look over this way

112

when your horse whinnied?"

"Relax, Ram. This is a ranch. Ranches have cattle and ranches have horses. Nothin' unusual about an animal makin' some noise on a full moon."

"Yeah," Ramsey grumbled. "I just wish I knew what was happening down there. Hell, we don't even know if Bolt's there."

"Patience my friend. Them injuns ain't gonna leave here till they get their revenge."

Chapter Eleven

Gray Wolf glanced at each of his braves. Each one nodded his readiness.

The braves moved quickly, their moccasins whispering across the wooden planks of the floor.

Gray Wolf and Turtle Belly dashed toward the girls in the chairs. Crooked Arrow ran to the left, stopped behind the sofa where the man and girl were too involved in their embrace to notice. Walking Stick shot off to the right and focused his attention on the girl in the long, gaudy red dress who played the piano. Bites Mad Dog took up his position a few feet inside the door, where he could keep an eye on everything in the room.

The blonde, Linda Ramsey, was the first to notice the Indians. She didn't turn her head away from the piano and look up until Gray Wolf was standing right next to her chair. She stared up at him for an instant, her eyes wide with surprise, her mouth slack.

Gray Wolf saw the heavy layer of powder and rouge on the pleasure girl's face and remembered the smooth, bronze complexion of his innocent sister. He saw the too-bright lipstick smeared on the whore's mouth and remembered the gag that bit into Plover Egg's and kept her from crying out for help.

He glanced down at the huge white breasts that spilled out over the top of the girls' low-cut dress. He thought about Plover Egg and, in his mind, he saw the white men mauling her small, young breasts with rough, grimy hands.

He glimpsed the bare flesh of the harlot's thigh, where the long slit in her green, silky dress fell open. And he thought of the bloody stains between Plover Egg's legs and hated the white men for brutally violating her most private part.

He saw the look of horror in the girls' wide, blue eyes. And he remembered the last time he'd seen his sister alive, when the filthy white man had ridden away, with the frightened Plover Egg huddled in front of him. He could still see the look of terror in his sister's soft brown eyes as Gray Wolf himself lay helpless on the ground, his mind falling down into some dark black hole.

Linda screamed when she saw the tomahawk in Gray Wolf's hand. He grabbed her by the arm and jerked her to her feet. She cringed, tried to pull away from him.

Turtle Belly moved in on the red-haired girl at the same time. He dashed around from the back of her chair, stood in front of her with his tomahawk poised to strike. He uttered a loud, guttural chant as he slashed down toward her throat. He stopped just short of nicking her flesh with the deadly weapon. Cathy Boring's shrill cry came right on top of Linda's.

Heads whirled around toward the middle of the room as if they'd been jerked simultaneously by invisible strings. For an instant, the others in the room were speechless as they watched Turtle Belly snatch Cathy's hair and pull her up out of the chair.

Harmony's hands froze in midair above the piano keys. She jumped up, ran toward the girls. "No! No!

115

Leave them alone!" she shouted.

Turtle Belly shot her a warning glare.

Harmony, who served as madam and housemother to the harlots, stopped abruptly when she saw the sudden movement to her left. She started to back away when she saw the older Indian coming toward her.

Winny Hart, the harlot who sat on the sofa with her lover, screamed, then buried her head in her hands. The customer sitting next to her, Paul Miles, a cowboy from another ranch, started to get up and reach for his gun. Crooked Arrow danced around to the front of the sofa and threatened the man with his tomahawk. Paul's hand eased away from his holster as he sank back down to the soft cushion.

The couple who were headed out the back door when the Indians entered the bordello, turned and started back down toward the room. George Harrison, the handsome man who wore a business suit, stopped midway in the dim hall, tugged on the arm of his harlot, pulled her into his arms. Doreen Jensen, the tallest of the four harlots, slapped her hands to her mouth, her eyes big as saucers as she stared at the attacking Indians. Her long, moaning wail, when it came, echoed throughout the entire house.

The lawyer brought his hand up to his chest, eased the hand inside the jacket.

Bites Mad Dog saw the movement in the dark hallway. He whipped out his bow, snatched an arrow from his quiver. In an instant, he had pulled back the bowstring, aimed at the man's chest.

Just before he released the arrow, the young Comanche remembered what Gray Wolf had said about not wanting this to turn into a massacre. He shifted his aim slightly, let the arrow fly before the man could draw his weapon.

The arrow zinged past the lawyer's head, twanged

116

into the wall behind him.

George Miles dropped to the floor, pulled the tall girl with him.

Bites Mad Dog whipped another arrow from his quiver, aimed the bow, and stood with his feet apart, daring the white man to go for his pistol again.

"Leave them alone!" Harmony yelled again. "Please don't hurt them." She put her hands to her mouth, backed up until she leaned against the wall next to the bar.

Walking Stick stepped closer to her, watched her with a careful eye, his tomahawk held in front of him.

Gray Wolf gripped Linda's arm as he glanced around the room and assessed the situation.

"Gather their guns," he told Turtle Belly in his native tongue. Gray Wolf stuffed his tomahawk in the band of his breechclout, then grabbed Cathy's arm and tightened his grasp around both girls.

Turtle Belly dashed to the sofa. He held his tomahawk in one hand, stretched the other out to the man who wore Levis, a clean shirt, and cowboy boots.

The burly customer understood the sign. With his fingers spread wide, Paul Miles kept one hand in the air, eased the pistol out of its holster with his thumb and forefinger. He brought the weapon up slowly, placed it on the Indian's open palm.

Turtle Belly shoved the gun in the band of his wide breechclout, then moved quickly to the man in the hall.

The dark, handsome lawyer looked at Turtle Belly's empty palm, then glared up at the Indian with contempt flashing in his dark eyes. George Harrison stuck his hand inside his coat, hesitated, as if he were weighing his chances of a quick-draw shot before the Indian could slash his hand with the sharp tomahawk. He glanced over at Bites Mad Dog and saw the young Comanche pull the bowstring back in a threatening gesture.

The lawyer slid the pistol out of its shoulder holster and relinquished it to Turtle Belly.

Turtle Belly tucked the small gun into his breech-clout band next to the other confiscated weapon and returned to take the red-haired harlot back from Gray Wolf.

The Indian braves had worked together as if they'd rehearsed the raid several times. In less than two minutes from the time they'd entered the building, they had secured their hostages without harming anyone else.

Satisfied that everything was in order, Gray Wolf put his tomahawk away and scooped the buxom harlot up in his arms. She was soft and weighed no more than a feather, he thought.

"Let me down!" Linda Ramsey screamed. "Let me down, you stinking redskin."

Linda's legs flailed the air as she tried desperately to fight off her attacker. She screamed and kicked, and raked her fingernails across Gray Wolf's cheeks in a frantic attempt to scratch out his eyes.

Blood oozed from the shallow scratches on Gray Wolf's flat cheeks. The little wounds brought him little pain. He tightened his grip on her arm and her leg where he held her in his arms.

"You are a fighting little tiger," Gray Wolf said in English as he smiled down in the girl's fiery eyes. He thought about his sister, Plover Egg, and wondered if she and Little Killdeer had tried to fight off their attackers so fiercely.

That was the part that bothered Gray Wolf. Thinking about the fear, the terror, that the two Indian maidens must have suffered when they were kidnapped, knowing what the white men would do to their innocent bodies.

118

"I'll kill you . . . you filthy beast!" Linda screamed as she pounded on his strong chest with small, ineffective fists.

Following Gray Wolf's lead, Turtle Belly lifted the other girl up in his arms.

Cathy Boring screamed hysterically as she struggled to free herself of the Indian's clutches. Her body trembled in the strong arms of her captor. She tried to hit him across the side of his head, but couldn't get enough leverage to do any damage. She reached up and grabbed a handful of black hair, tugged on it with all her might. But, again, the awkward angle of her arm kept her from pulling it hard enough to do any good.

"Help me, help me," the frightened girl cried as she covered her face with her hands and began to sob.

Walking Stick watched Harmony carefully as she slid behind the bar. Her elbow bumped against an empty glass, knocked it to the floor where it shattered with a tinkling crash.

She gave Walking Stick a dirty look, then looked over at Gray Wolf.

"You'd better put those girls down," she warned as her hand streaked under the counter. She brought up a small, loaded pistol, aimed it at Gray Wolf.

Walking Stick lunged toward her, knocked the weapon out of her hand. The pistol clattered to the floor and Walking Stick kicked it out into the room, then leaned over and picked it up.

"You filthy bastards! You'll never get away with this," Harmony shouted as she headed around the bar shaking her fists. "Put them down!" she demanded.

Walking Stick blocked her path.

Gray Wolf carried Linda toward the door.

Turtle Belly followed him, the girl in his arms sobbing, but no longer struggling.

The feisty girl in Gray Wolf's arms kicked and screamed and clawed at him with all of her strength. Gray Wolf let her struggle, knowing that she would wear herself out. He paused near the bar, stared at Harmony.

"We take your girls only to avenge the death of our own young women," he said in the white man's tongue. "Two of our girls die at the brutal hands of your white men. We now take two of your girls and kill them the same brutal way our women were murdered."

Linda's screams rang against Gray Wolf's ears as she thrashed about in his arms.

"No! No!" she cried as she reached up and tried to poke his eyes out.

Gray Wolf merely turned his head away.

Linda raised her head and bit Gray Wolf on the shoulder. He barely felt the sting of her teeth on his thick, tough skin.

Harmony tried to get to Gray Wolf but was blocked by the older Indian. "Our girls are not responsible for the death of your women. They have done nothing to hurt you. Why do you blame them?"

"I do not blame your women," Gray Wolf said in a cold voice.

"Then why do you have to take them?"

"Because it is the Comanche way."

"But why our girls?" Harmony pleaded. "Just leave them alone."

"Because Bolt and his friends took our Comanche women," Gray Wolf said in an even voice full of hatred.

"No, it isn't true," Harmony cried.

"You tell Bolt that we will do the same to his girls that he and his friends did to ours," Gray Wolf said. "He will know what I mean."

"What are you talking about?" Harmony demanded.

"We will rape these two girls and then kill them when

we have filled them with our seed. Just as Bolt and his filthy men did to our women."

Harmony was stunned by the Indian's words.

"No, you can't take our girls!" She yelled frantically. "It wasn't Bolt who did this terrible thing to your people. It was someone else. You're wrong about this. Bolt has never hurt a girl in his life. He just couldn't."

Gray Wolf ignored the woman's rantings.

"You tell Bolt that we take his women to avenge the deaths of our own," he said as he turned and headed for the door with the struggling girl in his arms.

"Stop! Stop!" Harmony shouted.

Gray Wolf paused, glanced over his shoulder at Harmony. "Another thing to tell your bastard friend," he said bitterly. "You tell Bolt that we will return. We will track him down and kill him to avenge another death besides our maidens."

"What do you mean?" Harmony frowned.

"Bolt and his friend killed our respected chief. Chief Yellow Dog. Bolt must pay for these unforgivable acts that he has committed against the members of our tribe."

"But he didn't do it," Harmony moaned. "I know he didn't."

"Yes," Gray Wolf said coldly. "Bolt did these things I tell you about. I saw him steal our maidens with my very own eyes. I fought with him. I saw his face up close. My mother saw him kill Chief Yellow Dog. These things I tell you are true."

"No, it isn't true," Harmony insisted. "Why do you think it was Bolt?"

"Because he told me his name."

"Then he told you wrong. I mean someone else told you wrong. I swear it wasn't Bolt. I know he wouldn't take your women. I know he wouldn't hurt any woman. He's not that way. He's a good man."

"If you think that, then you do not know him at all," Gray Wolf said. "He is a cruel, brutal man."

"Please don't take Linda and Cathy with you," Harmony begged. "Listen to me. Please. For God's sake, listen to me."

Gray Wolf would waste no more of his precious time arguing with the white woman. He and Turtle Belly dashed out the door with their hostages. As they ran toward their ponies, they heard the hysterical cries of the white women, the filthy curses of the men.

Bites Mad Dog stood just inside the door, his bow and arrow poised. "Go ahead," he told Walking Stick and Crooked Arrow. "I will cover for you."

The two older Indians backed slowly toward the door, their moccasins shuffling across the hardwood floor. They watched the others in the room with keen, darting eyes.

Bites Mad Dog pulled the bowstring back taut, threatening anyone who dared to move. He stood motionless at the doorway, ready to fire his arrow, until Crooked Arrow and Walking Stick were safely out of the room. And then the young Comanche waited another few minutes to give the braves a chance to get to their horses.

Then Bites Mad Dog turned and ran for his life, his breechclout flapping at his bare, bronze ass.

Harmony was the first one to run to the door. Paul Miles left Winny Hart crying on the couch and dashed up behind Harmony. An instant later, the handsome lawyer, George Harrison, came running up from the hallway, dragging Doreen Jensen by the hand.

"They're gone," Harmony cried as she saw the Indians ride away into the darkness. She clapped her hands to her cheeks. "Do something! Quick!"

But, already, Harmony knew they were too late.

"You hear that?" said Hutch.

"What?" asked Jack Ramsey.

"The screams."

Jack Ramsey listened for a moment. "Yeah, I hear it. Good. Now we've got some action." The outlaw leader smiled, please with himself because his plan was working so well.

"Wish I could have seen the look on Bolt's face when those fuckin' injuns raided the whorehouse," he laughed.

"Maybe Bolt ain't there," Hutch said as he peered into the darkness.

Ramsey ignored the remark. He had his own thoughts.

"Damn, I wish we were close enough to see the injuns murder that son of a bitch," he sneered. "It'd give me great pleasure to watch that bastard squirm."

"Shut up, Ram. I'm trying to listen."

Ramsey stuffed the last big chunk of chewing tobacco in his mouth and leaned back against the tree. For the next few minutes, the two heartless outlaws stood in total silence as the moon spread a thin, ghostly layer of silver across the vast Texas landscape.

Somewhere on a distant hill, a coyote yapped. Two other coyotes answered his call.

Restless, Ramsey pushed away from the tree, paced a slow circle around the clump of trees as he scanned the countryside for the dozenth time.

A cow in a nearby field bawled its discomfort. Several others took up the bellowing moan.

"Damn those cattle," grumbled Ramsey as he walked back to his original position by the tree. He spit a stream of tobacco juice to the ground.

"Damn those cattle," he grumbled.

"It's that damned full moon that's making them

edgy," Hutch said.

Ramsey knew what Hutch meant. The full moon was making him edgy, too. He felt the tenseness in his shoulder muscles, the knot that tightened in his gut, the apprehension that crawled through his veins. Even when he tried to take slow, deep breaths to calm himself, Ramsey felt the muscles in his chest tauten with an uneasiness that he couldn't explain away.

He spit the wad of tobacco to the ground and already felt the pangs of wanting more, knowing that he couldn't get more tobacco until they got to San Antonio. His patience was running thin. He leaned back against the rough bark of the tree and closed his eyes. He didn't know why he was so nervous. He had nothing to fear. Hell, he'd done his part in this thing. It was just the waiting that got him, he decided. The not knowing.

Except for an occasional bawl from one of the cattle, the night became quiet again.

"There they go now," Hutch said a few minutes later. He stepped out from the cluster of trees on the dark hill and pointed toward the fleeing Indians in the distance.

Ramsey squinted, peered across the land. He could just barely make out the dim silhouettes of the horsemen.

"I wonder if they killed Bolt," he said.

"You don't know Comanches very well, do you?" Hutch said. "They don't leave a place unless they've taken care of what they came to do."

"Yeah, I guess you're right. I didn't hear any gunshots, though."

"Indians don't kill with guns, you big jerk," Hutch chided. "They use bows and arrows and their trusty tomahawks."

"I know that. I just thought Bolt would put up a good fight."

"Comanches are known for their surprise attacks," Hutch assured him. "Hell, those bastards can sneak up on a crowd of men and snatch every goddamned scalp in sight and still be twenty miles away before anyone knows they were there."

"So I've heard. Let's just hope to hell they got Bolt's scalp."

"It looks like one of them is carrying a passenger," Hutch said as he squinted his eyes and strained to see. "Can't tell for sure, but they must be taking Bolt with them."

"Good," Ramsey spit. "Maybe they'll burn him at the stake."

"You want to ride down to the bordello and check it out?" Hutch suggested.

"Hell, no. I don't want to arouse their suspicions by showin' my face."

"Then let's get the hell out of here."

"Yeah," Ramsey grinned. "We got some celebratin' to do."

Chapter Twelve

Tom was out of breath when he ran into the brothel. When he'd heard the screams, he'd dashed out the back door and run down the hill as fast as he could, almost tripping over his own feet.

"What's wrong? I heard the screams," he panted.

Harmony Sanchez ran up to Tom, threw her arms around him, and started crying.

"Oh, Tom, they've stolen our girls!"

"Who's stolen them?"

"Indians. Comanches, I think. There were five of them," she said as she looked up at Tom.

Tom patted her on the back, looked across the room and saw Doreen and Winny huddled on the sofas, the two men who tried to comfort them.

"Who'd they get? Linda and Cathy?" He pushed Harmony away and dashed over to the twin sofas.

"Yes. It was just awful," she cried as she trotted after Tom. "It happened so quick. They took our guns, and we couldn't defend ourselves. Oh, those poor girls. They're going to kill them."

"Calm down, Harmony," Tom said when he saw that she was hysterical. He grabbed her by the shoulders, forced her to be still. "Did you see which way they went?"

"They headed toward the river when they left here," George Harrison said. "But no telling which way they'll go."

Winny's shoulders heaved with wracking sobs. Paul Miles sat on the sofa beside her, his arm around her as he tried to comfort her.

"They . . . they . . . had tom . . . toma—tomahawks," Winny sobbed.

"Take it easy, Winny." Paul wrapped both arms around the girl, drew her close, rubbed the back of her head.

"Find them. Please find them, Tom," Doreen pleaded. "Before they . . . before they hurt Linda and Cathy."

When she looked up at Tom, he saw that her eyes were red-rimmed, puffy.

"I'll do what I can, Doreen," he assured her. "Harmony, get these girls a shot of whiskey."

"I . . . I can't. I can't even think. Oh, those poor girls," she wailed.

Tom grabbed Harmony by the shoulders and shook her gently until she calmed down.

"Get a hold of yourself," he said sternly. If we're going to find Linda and Cathy, I'm gonna need your help. Where in the hell is Bolt?"

"I don't know. He never came back," Harmony said.

"Damn! I want to know what happened. Harmony, get that whiskey for the girls," he ordered. "And get one for yourself."

Paul Miles made Winny comfortable on the sofa, told her he'd be right back, then walked across the room with Harmony to help her with the drinks.

George Harrison stood up and quickly told Tom the details of the raid.

Harmony and Paul Miles brought the small tumblers of whiskey over and Paul helped the girls drink it.

"You say they were Comanches?" Tom said as he stared down at the floor.

"That's what they said. The arrow's still hanging from the wall back there, if that'll help."

Tom and George walked to the hallway in the back of the house. Tom jerked the arrow free, took it back to the living room where he leaned over and held the shaft under the light of a coal-oil lamp. He examined the flint arrowhead, twirled the arrow in his hands as he studied the short, trimmed, black and red feathers on the other end.

"Looks like a Comanche arrow, but I can't be sure." Tom set the arrow down on the table, next to the lamp, walked back over to the girls.

"They insisted that it was Bolt and a friend of Bolt's who killed their women," Harmony said. "Why would they think such a thing?"

"And their chief," George Harrison added. "The Indians accused Bolt of killing their chief. Chief Yellow Dog, I think."

"Yellow Dog, I've heard the name." Tom shook his head. "It doesn't make sense. Unless someone's got a grudge against Bolt and this is their way of getting even."

"What do you mean, Tom?" Doreen asked.

"I mean you don't go around killing an Indian chief and stealing his women and then announce who you are by telling them your name."

"Does Bolt have any enemies?" Harrison asked.

"Not that I know of," Tom said. "An old bounty hunter, maybe. No, I don't know."

Harmony suddenly clutched at his arms. The expression in her eyes was full of fear and desperation.

"Tom, what if they've already killed Bolt? What if the Indians killed him before they came here?"

Tom reached up and took her hands from his

128

shoulders, held them in his own hands.

"Look, Harmony. It's all very confusing right now. But we're not getting anywhere with all this second-guessing. I've got to go and see what I can find out. Damn, I wish Bolt were here."

"I'll go with you," offered George Harrison.

"Me, too," said Paul Miles.

"Good. Harmony, you've got a couple of spare pistols upstairs, don't you?"

"Yes, three of them. We keep them hidden in the dresser drawers in the bedrooms. Just in case."

"Will you run up and get them?"

When Harmony returned, Tom took two of the guns, gave them to the other men, and told Harmony to keep the third one handy.

Winny reached up and grabbed Tom's hand.

"Don't go, Tom," she begged. "Please don't leave us alone. The Indians might come back."

"George, you'd better stay with the girls," Tom said. "Paul and I'll ride out to the ridge and see if we can find anything. If not, we'll come right back and I'll go looking for Bolt."

Tom checked his gun, shoved it back in its holster. He walked over behind the counter, grabbed a bunch of sulphur matches that were kept there to light the lanterns and candles. On his way out of the bordello, he took the binoculars off the peg near the door and slung the strap over his shoulder.

"Be careful," Harmony said.

"I will," Tom smiled.

Tom was glad the moon was full that night as he and Paul rode along the ridges and valleys of the rolling hills out behind the ranch. There were just too damned many places a man could hide on the property. He saw the tracks when he got to one of the two gates at the back forty, but that didn't mean anything to Tom. He and Bolt and the other ranch hands used that gate almost every day when the rode the fence line.

He hopped down, opened the gate, led his horse through, then waited for Paul Miles to ride through before he closed it.

"We'll ride out to that far hill," Tom said as he mounted his horse again. "From there you can see for miles."

The two men rode straight out across the flat fields where the wild grasses were tall this time of year. When they got to the crest of the hill, they reined up on their horses.

Tom scanned the flat, moonlit landscape with his naked eye, turning slowly in his saddle. He saw odd, ghostly silhouettes where he knew there were trees. He saw the familiar boulder straight ahead. He paid particular attention to the trees on the other side of the river, but nothing seemed out of place.

Except for the night singing of crickets, a yapping of a coyote, there were no unfamiliar sounds. He brought the binoculars up to his eyes, checked the land more closely, then let the binoculars fall back on the strap that he had around his neck. His head turned slowly as he checked the land one last time.

Tom's heart fluttered when he thought he saw a small group of riders way to the south of them. He studied it with his eyes for a moment and swore he could see it moving. The binoculars didn't do much good at night, but using them again, he saw that the silhouette was nothing more than a cluster of cottonwoods. He was disappointed.

"Think we'd better head back," he said.

They turned and rode straight back toward the ranch, slowed down when they neared the edge of the property.

"Think they'll go very far tonight?" Paul asked as

they rode along the fence line, just beyond Bolt's property.

"Depends on what they got in mind. Something's not clicking right about this whole deal, but I can't put my finger on it."

They hadn't ridden very far when Tom's horse faltered a little. Tom glanced down and saw the wide depression in the ground, the moonlight glittering off the loose rocks and stones.

"Hold up," he said. "That hole wasn't here early this morning when I was out this way checking the fences."

Both men slid off their horses, leaned over the shallow hole. Tom pulled a few matches out of his pocket, struck one on a rock. He held it above the depression, moved it around.

"Looks like somebody started to dig a grave here, but they got scared off before they finished it," Tom said.

"Maybe they just got discouraged," Paul said. "There's a hell of a lot of rocks in there. It wouldn't be easy diggings."

Tom spotted something just as the match burned down to his finger. He blew it out, tossed it down, struck another one. He picked up the scrap of material that was shaped like a matchstick, then found another one. He examined it, felt the texture.

"Looks like a piece of hide," he told Paul.

"Buckskin," Paul said after he'd looked at both pieces. "Fringe from a man's shirt?"

"Or a woman's dress. An Indian woman's dress."

"What're you thinking?" Paul asked.

"I don't know yet, but I got a feeling that Indian gals were buried here today, sometime after I was out here this morning."

"They're not here now."

Tom examined the hole more thoroughly, went

through a dozen matches. Finally, he found a few long strands of black hair. He held them close to the match.

"Horse hair or Indian hair?" he asked.

"Your guess is as good as mine."

"I got a hunch these came from those two Indian girls Bolt was supposed to have killed."

"I think you're right."

"Shallow grave. Right behind our property," Tom thought out loud. "Out in the open like this, where it would be easy for the Indians to find it."

"You're sayin' that somebody led those Indians here to Bolt's ranch."

"That's what I'm thinkin'," said Tom.

"But why?"

"That's what puzzles me. Let's look around."

Stooped over like little old ladies, Tom and Paul searched the ground. They spread out, away from the grave, walked in opposite directions.

"There are a lot of hoofprints around here that don't belong to us. Must have been a gang of riders," Tom observed.

"The Indian who spoke English said that he saw Bolt and his friend steal the women," Paul said. "But later, he said Bolt and his men, plural."

"Sounds like somebody had this all planned out."

"Indians don't chew tobacco, do they?" Paul asked a minute later.

"Not that I know of." Tom stood up straight, looked over at Paul who was walking toward him.

"Here, smell this." Paul shoved a damp glob of brown stuff under Tom's nose.

"Yep. That's tobacco."

They searched a little while longer and Tom came up with a few cigarette butts, then found a small, empty whiskey bottle that had been tossed over by a tree.

"Not much to go on," he said as he placed the long

132

strands of dark hair and the cigarette butts in his shirt pocket, then shoved the empty whiskey bottle in his pants pocket.

"You want the wad of tobacco, too?" Paul asked.

"Thanks, but no thanks. We'd better get back. I've got to see if I can find Bolt."

"Who'd do a thing like this?" Paul asked as they rode back to the ranch.

"Somebody who's got a great big bone to pick with Bolt."

●

"I'm ready to tie one on tonight," said Kyle Hutchinson.

"Yeah, I could use a good stiff belt right about now," said Jack Ramsey. "To tell you the truth, though, I'd settle for a great big drink of water. That heat today really dried me out."

"Not to mention all the traveling we did," Hutch laughed. "We should have filled our canteens at the river before we left."

"I wasn't really thinking about water right then. We'll be all right. It isn't that far to town."

"I reckon Oppie's feelin' no pain by now."

"I don't worry about him," Ramsey said, "as long as he doesn't drink when we're working. He's probably asleep by now and that's what I'm gonna do. I'm gonna have one drink with you and the boys and then I'm gonna find me a room for the night. This day has taken it all out of me."

The two outlaws were in no particular hurry to get to San Antonio. They'd run their horses pretty hard that day and they now allowed them to set their own pace.

"I'm glad the moon's full tonight," Hutch said.

"You wouldn't be scared of the dark, would you, Hutch?" Ramsey chided.

"Sure. Aren't you?"

"Hutch, do you really think that was Bolt they were carrying with them when the Indians hightailed it out of there?"

"I don't know. It wasn't one of them, that's for sure. There were seven horses and seven Indians when they came, and best I could tell, there were seven horses and eight riders when they left."

"Hutch, you don't suppose . . ."

Hutch waited, then turned to his friend.

"I don't suppose what?"

"It didn't dawn on me at the time, but you don't suppose they stole one of Holt's harlots, do you?" Ramsey hadn't thought about that possibility when he'd conjured up this elaborate scheme to get Bolt. He grew sick when he thought about it.

"You ain't thinkin' they took Linda, are you?"

"It's possible."

"Anything's possible. Why would they want to take one of the girls? You set it up so they'd go after Bolt, and obviously, that's what they did."

"Indians have a thing about an eye for an eye. God, I hope they don't have Linda."

"If that's your line of thinking," Hutch said, "then why wouldn't they steal two girls?"

"Maybe they did. Maybe you just didn't see the other one."

"I think you're making too much out of this, Ram."

"But what if they've got Linda?"

"What if? Do you want to turn around and chase after the injuns?"

"If it were your sister . . ."

"Look, Ram, don't worry about it. I'm not sure the Indians had anyone with them at all when they left. The dark plays strange tricks on your eyes, you know. Besides that, they were so damned far away from us, I could just barely see them."

"Yeah, I know."

The two men rode in silence for a while. Ramsey knew he was edgy tonight. It was just that goddamned unknown fear cropping up again. The not knowing for sure.

"Listen, what was that?" Ramsey said.

"What? I didn't hear anything."

Ramsey cocked his head, listened.

"Wagon wheels. Or a buggy. Someone's coming this way from town," he said.

"Well, this is the main road to San Antone. Seems reasonable that someone would be using it."

"Yeah, I'm just edgy tonight."

"You're lettin' the full moon get to you," Hutch laughed.

"Yeah. I never believed that about the full moon making you crazy, but I'm beginning to wonder."

"You want to ride off the road until the buggy passes by?" Hutch suggested.

"No," snapped Ramsey. "Hell, I ain't got nothin' to hide."

The clattering of wagon wheels got louder, and finally Ramsey could see the buckboard up ahead of them. When it got closer, he could see the dark outlines of the driver and the passenger.

"Just a couple of lovers out for a moonlit ride." Ramsey heaved a sigh of relief.

"Boy, you are jumpy tonight."

As the buckboard approached them, Ramsey didn't turn to look, but stared straight ahead.

"Good evening, gentlemen," called the driver of the buckboard as it passed right by them.

"Howdy," Hutch called back politely.

Still, Ramsey stared straight ahead, ignored the couple in the buckboard.

A hundred yards down the road, Hutch turned to look at Ramsey.

"Have you lost your manners, Ram? You were downright rude to those people."

"Not rude. I just didn't want to get into a conversation with them, that's all."

"You mean you were feeling guilty about what you did today and you were afraid they'd know just by looking at you."

"No, it wasn't that. I just didn't feel like talking." Ramsey knew damned well that Hutch was right. He didn't want those people looking at him too close. That, and because he didn't want to be seen leaving the scene of a crime. He didn't want anyone noticing him at all.

"Look, if you want to draw attention to yourself, you just did it with your rudeness. A simple 'howdy' would have been the polite thing to do."

Ramsey sulked. He knew that Hutch was always right. And he knew the difference between the two of them. Hutch had no fear at all.

Chapter Thirteen

The flat road stretched out ahead of them like a pale silver ribbon. The buckboard clanked and clattered as it bounced along the moonlit trail.

"That one fellow was downright rude," Mary Beth Piper said after they had passed the two riders who were heading toward town.

"Better rude than vicious." Bolt turned and smiled at Mary. She had close beside him on the cushioned seat of the buckboard.

"You wouldn't be trying to scare me, would you, Bolt?" She smiled at him coyly, snuggled in closer.

Bolt liked the feel of her warm body next to his. He felt comfortable with Mary and had enjoyed the day they'd spent together. He hadn't meant to be gone from the ranch so long, but after dinner and a stroll through town, they had gone up to her room and made love again. And now, he was in no hurry to get home.

"If scaring you is going to make you sit closer, then maybe I am," he grinned. "But, seriously, you never know who you're going to run into out here. This road gets pretty lonely at night."

"You mean that could have been robbers we just passed?" she said.

"Or worse. Robbers, outlaws, hardcases. Even murderers. They all use this road, same as you and I. And types like that, they like to travel at night. That's why I'm always polite when I meet someone out here at night. Doesn't pay to be rude to the wrong fellow."

Bolt felt her body tremble.

"Oh, Bolt, I wish you hadn't said that. Now I really am scared."

"What's to be scared about? The hardcases don't bother you. They just want to ride right on by without you checking them over."

"But those men might have been murderers," she said, her voice almost a whisper.

"They might have been, but they didn't bother us, did they?" He slid his hand over to her thigh, squeezed her. Don't worry about such things. I'm not going to let anyone hurt you."

"Oh, Bolt, you're so brave."

"Not brave, I just don't go lookin' for trouble. And I don't spend my time worrying about something that'll never happen." He felt her body relax against him.

"Bolt, do you ever get scared?"

"Darned right I do. When there's a reason to be scared. And right now there's no reason."

He leaned over and kissed her gently on the mouth, felt her soft, pliant lips give under his. Her delicate scent seemed to float on the air all around him and he felt heady. She slid her tongue inside his mouth, and he wanted her again.

He pulled slowly away from her, took in a deep breath, and sat up straight again.

"Is that all I get? One kiss?" she pouted.

"It's mighty hard to kiss you and steer the buggy at the same time," he teased.

"Then, why don't you stop it?"

"Mary Beth, you'd wear a man out."

"Bolt, was I good for you?"

"Yes, you were good for me." He switched the reins to the other hand, put his arm around her shoulder, and drew her closer. She settled down against him and put her head on his shoulder. "You're beautiful in bed."

"So are you. I wondered what it would be like to have a man make love to me, and you made me feel better than anything I could have imagined."

"I'm glad."

"This moonlight night is so romantic," she sighed. Her hand slid over to his crotch.

"Bolt, you know that little cottage where you said I could stay?"

"Yeah."

"Could you spend the night with me?"

"I could," he grinned.

"I wouldn't want to break any rules."

"You're not working for me, are you?"

"No."

"Then there aren't any rules."

Bolt kissed her again, this time long and deep and lingering. Her hand squeezed the bulge in his pants, then began massaging it. His stalk began to grow beneath the warmth of her hand.

"Oh, Bolt, I want you again," she husked when she broke the kiss. She slid her hand inside his pants, took his growing stalk in her hand.

"I want you, too. I really do. But I think we'd better wait until we get to the ranch. I know Tom will be wondering about me by now."

"I understand. I can wait."

But Bolt couldn't. He pulled the wagon way off the road, pulled back on the reins.

"To hell with it," he said. "Tom can handle things at the ranch."

Tom wore a long face when he and Paul returned from looking for the Indians.

"Isn't Bolt back yet?" he asked.

"No," Harmony said. "Did you find anything?"

"No, not a trace of those damned Indians." Tom didn't want to mention the grave that he and Paul had discovered in front of the girls. Winny and Doreen were already too badly shaken by what had happened and he didn't think they could handle anything else just yet. He walked across the room with Paul to check on them.

"They've settled down," George Harrison said.

"Didn't you find Linda and Cathy?" asked Doreen. She sat up and looked at Tom with sad, red-rimmed eyes.

"No, but we will," Tom assured her. "Don't you worry about it."

"I can't help but worry."

"I know, but everything's going to be all right."

"I hope nothing's happened to them," said Winny from the other sofa as she sat up to make room for Paul. But Paul didn't sit down.

"We'll find them," Tom said again.

"You want me to ride into town and see if I can find Bolt?" Paul offered.

"You may have to, but wait until I get my thoughts together."

The front door creaked open.

Tom spun around, slid his hand down to his holster, where his hand hovered over the butt of his pistol. He saw Harmony bring a smaller pistol out of her pocket and aim it at the doorway. An instant later, he saw her relax and slip the gun back in her pocket as two nicely-groomed men walked through the doorway.

Tom recognized the men, too. Ralph and Dale Rader, brothers and co-owners of the barbershop in

San Antonio, were regular customers at the bordello.

"Why the gun, Harmony?" Dale laughed. "Is this a holdup?"

"No. We've had a little trouble here tonight," Harmony said solemnly.

"Oh, sorry to hear that?" Ralph said. "Anything serious?"

"Yeah, it was pretty bad," Tom said as he walked over to the Rader brothers. "The girls won't be working tonight. Sorry."

Both bothers glanced over at the girls and the men who were with them.

"Are they sick?" Ralph asked.

"No," said Harmony. "Just not feeling well."

Ralph shrugged his shoulders.

"Well, could we get a drink while we're here?" he asked. "It's a long ride back to town."

"Yeah," said Tom. "Harmony, get them something to drink, will you?"

"Sure." Harmony went around behind the bar, set two tumblers in front of the brothers. She poured a shot of whiskey in each one.

"Thanks," they said in unison. They turned on their barstools to face Tom.

"So, what happened here?" Ralph asked after he'd taken a big swallow of whiskey.

"Indians raided us," Tom said.

"Oh, my God, no. Did anybody get hurt?" Dale asked with a genuine concern. He glanced over at the twin sofas again.

Tom felt a knot form in the pit of his stomach, his muscles tighten. He stared at the floor, paced a few steps before he answered.

"No," he said. "Well, we don't know. The Indians took Linda and Cathy with them."

"Oh, that's terrible. I'm so sorry," Ralph said. "Is

there anything we can do to help?"

"No, I don't think so. We're gonna track the bastards down and get the girls back as soon as Bolt gets here. Paul and I went out looking for them shortly after it happened, but those Indians were gone. Just plain gone." Tom paced back and forth.

"Were they Comanches?" Dale asked.

"Yeah. I think so."

"Hell, Comanches are the best damned horsemen there are," said Ralph.

"I know. They must be riding like hell."

Tom sat down on the high barstool between the brothers and they swung around to face him.

"You know, it won't be easy tracking those Comanches," Dale said in a low voice so that Winny and Doreen couldn't hear him. "You ought to get yourself up a posse."

"We probably will," Tom said. He tapped his fingers nervously on the countertop.

"You want a drink, Tom?" Harmony offered.

"No thanks."

He raised his hands to his head, rubbed his temples where the tension was the worst. He curled his fingers to hard fists and slammed them down on the countertop.

"Damn it! Where in the hell is Bolt?" he yelled.

"Someone mention my name?" Bolt grinned as he came through the door with Mary.

Tom jumped up. "Damn it, Bolt! Where in the hell have you been?"

"Well, that's a fine way to greet me." Bolt felt the tension in the room then, saw the look on Tom's face. He glanced around and saw the somber faces. He got sick inside.

"Hey, why all the long faces? What happened," he asked.

"Bolt, we got trouble. Big trouble. The Indians got Linda and Cathy?"

"What? God, no! How? When?"

"Just sit down and listen to me for a minute," Tom said.

The Radar brothers scooted down to the end barstools to make room for Bolt and Mary. George Harrison walked over and stood near the bar.

"Go ahead and sit down, Mary," Bolt said, then took a seat beside her. "What happened, Tom?"

Tom purposely didn't tell Bolt about the shallow grave at the edge of their property, but gave him a quick rundown on the events of the raid.

Anger boiled up inside of him as Tom talked, but he didn't interrupt. He saw Mary put her hands to her face, wipe her eyes.

"Why'd they take the girls?" he asked when Tom paused for breath.

Harmony explained what Gray Wolf had told her about avenging the deaths of the Indian women and the Comanche chief.

"That's nonsense," Bolt said.

"We know it is," Tom said, "but it doesn't help our situation."

"Damn! I wish I'd been here." Bolt stood up and fought back the tears, the guilt.

Tom put his hand on Bolt's shoulder.

"It wouldn't have helped, Bolt," he said gently. "I was up at the house when it happened, and since it was early evening, you would have been up there, too. You couldn't have gotten down here any faster than I did. I came running when I heard the first scream and the damned Indians were gone before I got here."

"They were here only two minutes, at the most," said Harrison. "It happened so quick. They caught us off guard and we just didn't have a chance."

"Did they . . ." Bolt glanced over at the girls on the sofas. "Did they hurt Winny and Doreen?"

"No," said Harrison. "The Indians didn't do anything except sneak into the room, go straight for Linda and Cathy, grab them up and keep us from fighting back. And then, like Tom said, they were gone."

"Yeah," said Tom. "They disappeared into thin air."

"It doesn't make sense. Any of it," Bolt said. "Well, Tom, we've got to get moving. Right away."

Ralph Rader stood up. "I think we'd better be getting out of your way," he said, "unless there's anything we can do to help you."

"We'll ride with you, if you want," said Dale Rader.

"No thanks," said Bolt. "I think Tom and I can make it faster by ourselves. We know the country around here like the backs of our hands."

"Well, good luck," Dale said and the two Rader brothers departed.

"The Indians can't be more than half an hour ahead of us," Tom said. "I'll fill you in on my theories about this while we're riding."

"Good," said Bolt. "By the way, Harmony, this is Mary Beth Piper. Will you take care of her? I told her she could sleep in one of the cottages."

"Hi, Mary Beth," Harmony said. "We'll take care of you."

"Let's get our things together," Bolt said.

"Paul and I will stay here with the girls until you get back," said George Harrison, "so don't worry about them while you're gone."

"Thanks, George," Bolt said. His mind worked frantically, trying to think of the things they'd need. "Paul, could you go out to the stable and saddle my horse? Saddlebags, too. Put the buckboard in the barn later."

"Sure," Paul said.

"Harmony, have you got any beef jerky in here?"

Harmony reached under the counter and grabbed a package that was wrapped in butcher paper, handed it to Bolt.

"We might need jackets. And matches," Bolt said as he thought of the things. "The binoculars. Paul, put the bedroll on my horse. Bring Tom's bedroll up, too, and he can tie it down. Anything else we need?"

"The saddlebags are already packed," Tom said. "There's some food in them, ammunition. Is your canteen full?"

"It's out in the buckboard. Think it needs water. Better take an extra canteen along. No telling where those bastards are."

Paul left for the stable. Harrison dashed up to the house to get Bolt's and Tom's jackets. Tom grabbed the binoculars from the peg by the door, put the strap over his shoulder. Harmony scurried around the house, gathered up things she thought they would need.

Fifteen minutes later, Bolt and Tom were ready to go.

"Be careful," Harmony said.

"We will," Bolt said.

"Please bring Linda and Cathy back," Doreen said as she got up from the couch.

"We will," Bolt assured her.

Bolt and Tom dashed out the door, jumped on their horses, and headed for the back of the property.

The others gathered just outside the door and watched them go, then, when they could no longer see them, went back inside and bolted the door shut.

As Bolt and Tom rode across the field, Tom explained about the grave and the things he'd found there. He told him about the tobacco wad that was still damp.

"You were set up, Bolt." Tom said. "Hell, somebody led those Indians right up to your back door."

"It looks that way. But who did it?"

"Somebody who's got a big grudge against you."

"I can't think of anybody who hates my guts enough to pull a vicious stunt like this. I mean, this is a pretty sick way to get revenge." Bolt shook his head.

"You'd better start thinking pretty damned hard, 'cause from what I can tell, catching the Indians and getting the girls back isn't gonna end our problems."

"I think you're right. Thank God the moon's full. Having that light is going to help us a lot."

"It will," said Tom. "But it's also a disadvantage. The moonlight works both ways. It'll make it easier for us to see the Indians, but it'll also make it easier for them to see us."

"We'll ride careful."

"There's the grave, right over there," Tom pointed. "Just down a ways from the gate."

"Yeah, I can see it from here."

"You want to stop and have a look-see?"

"Just for a minute. I don't want to waste any time."

Tom hopped down, opened the gate, closed it after they were both through it. They rode along the fence line until they came to the grave. They both slid off their horses, leaned over the shallow depression, and struck matches.

A cow bawled in the nearby pasture.

The noise startled Bolt for just an instant.

A second later, Bolt heard another sound. He blew out his match.

"Listen," he whispered.

Tom extinguished the flame on his match, dropped it to the ground. Both men stayed perfectly still.

Bolt heard it again. The crunching of twigs, the fast, faint hoofbeats, coming from the direction where he and Tom had just been riding.

"Somebody's coming," he whispered. He scanned the

146

silvery hills, saw nothing out of place. "Quick. Hide in the trees."

The men drew their pistols, tucked themselves up against two nearby trees.

The hoofbeats got louder.

And then Bolt saw the lone horseman rise over the nearby ridge. The rider kept to the cover of the line of trees, slowed down when the horse came over the ridge.

The horse kept coming. Slower, as if the rider were trying to sneak up on them. But Bolt knew that he and Tom had the advantage.

"I told you it was a trap," Tom whispered.

That's when the sweat broke on Bolts' forehead.

He tensed and glanced all around him, searched for the other ambushers.

Chapter Fourteen

Bolt glimpsed the dark outline of the rider briefly, near the row of trees. Closer this time. And then the rider dropped out of sight. Vanished. Nothing.

No sound. No hoofbeats. No crunching of twigs or mesquite bushes. No cows bawling. No night birds singing. Dead silence. Nothing. Nothing but the loud pounding of Bolt's chest.

He was afraid to whisper to Tom. He was afraid to turn his head and look around him. His eyes darted back and forth in their sockets. Nothing. Nothing but the pounding of his heart.

A fence post creaked. As if somebody had leaned against it. Or climbed over it.

He turned his head only slightly to look up and down the fence line.

And then he saw it.

The head sticking up over the top of the fence. The eyes that glittered in the moonlight like a cat's in darkness. The long black hair.

No sound. Nothing except the pounding in his chest and the shadowy face, the glittering eyes that peered at him over the wire fence.

Bolt eased the hammer back, cursed the click.

And then the whispered voice came out of the

darkness and scared Bolt half to death.

"Bolt?" said the soft, whispered voice.

Female, he was sure.

"Who is it?" Bolt whispered back.

"Mary. Mary Beth."

Bolt exhaled the breath he'd been holding, blew it out in a big sigh.

"What the hell are you doing here?" He eased the hammer back down, slid the gun into the holster. He opened the gate for Mary. When she came through, he saw the black scarf she wore over her blond hair.

"Jeez. You scared us to death," Tom said with a big sigh.

Mary threw her arms around Bolt's neck, held on for dear life.

"Oh, Bolt, I'm so frightened."

"Well, so are we. Now," Bolt said sarcastically, annoyed that she had followed them. Now he'd have to take her back to the ranch and lose precious time. "You almost got yourself shot."

"I had to come. I want to go with you."

"You can't ride with us, Mary. It's just too damned dangerous. Where'd you get the horse?"

"I borrowed him," she said meekly.

"From whom?" Bolt demanded.

"The horse was out in front of the bordello. I think it belongs to one of those fellows back there."

"Dammit, Mary, you can't go with us. You'll slow us down."

"No I won't. I promise. I'm good on a horse."

"But you just can't go with us. You've got to ride back to the house."

"I was afraid to stay at that little cottage by myself, after what happened there."

"Harmony didn't tell you to sleep out in the cottage, did she?"

149

"No, I just figured—"

"Well, you figured wrong, dammit. Harmony would have insisted that you sleep upstairs in the living quarters of the bordello, where the rest of them sleep. Now you get on your horse and ride your sweet ass back there."

"No," she begged. "I'm afraid to stay there. I want to be with you. I won't go back."

"Then I'll have to waste my time and drag you back there myself."

"I'd just follow you again."

"Dammit, Mary, you're the most pigheaded woman I've ever known."

"You called me that before," she giggled.

"Don't be sweet. It won't do you any good this time," Bolt accused unfairly.

"Well, I'm going with you and that's that."

"I'm furious with you, Mary, but if you want to tag along, go right ahead. But, I'll tell you this right now, little lady. You're on your own. Tom and I go at our own pace, which is going to be pretty damned fast. If you can't keep up, you find your own way back home."

"I'll keep up with you."

"Stubborn bitch!"

"Names don't hurt me."

"I'm sorry, Mary. But we're talking about the lives of two of my girls. They mean as much to me as if they were my own sister and I'm not going to let them down."

"I understand. I'll help you all I can."

"Just stay out of our way and that'll be a big help. And you follow every damned order I give you."

"Yes, sir," she snapped. "I can cook for you," she said in a nicer tone.

"This ain't no picnic we're going on. We've got jerky and very little else. You eat that or you eat grass. Your

150

choice."

"I will."

"And there won't be any cook fires. No fires at all. Do you understand?"

"I'm stronger than you think I am."

"We'll see, but don't expect us to bail you out if you go soft on us."

"I won't."

"Let's get moving before we're too late."

Mary ran back and untied her horse from the tree near the fence. By the time she got back to the gate and bolted it shut, Bolt and Tom were a hundred feet ahead of her. She jerked the reins, caught up with them quickly, then fell in behind them.

Bolt glanced back when he sensed her behind him. The moonlight glimmered off the moist lips of her smile. Without returning her smile, he turned his head and looked straight ahead.

"Bolt?" she called after a few minutes.

Bolt whirled around in the saddle, shot her a dirty look.

"No talking while we're riding," he ordered. "You want to let the Indians know we're coming?"

She didn't answer.

"Do you understand me?"

Still no answer. He saw her sit up tall in the saddle, saw her turn her head and scan the landscape. He turned around and chuckled to himself. Stubborn as she was, Mary probably wouldn't utter another word the whole damned trip. Which was just the way Bolt wanted it.

Fess Grodin noticed the two men who came through the swinging batwing doors. Almost everyone in the saloon did. They men were dressed better than any man in the place and they looked enough alike to be identical twins.

Fess turned away when he saw them coming toward the bar.

The Rader brothers slid onto the empty barstools next to Fess. They smelled like barbershops, Fess thought. Shaving lather and lye soap. He studied their reflections in the gilded mirror behind the bar, fascinated by their neat appearance. There was only so much he could stare at, and after a couple of minutes, he lost his interest. He turned and glanced around the saloon, as he had done several times since he came in.

Fess couldn't understand where the other members of his gang were. Except for Ramsey and Hutch, who were still out at the ranch when they first got to town, the other five had gone straight to the new River Front Hotel down the street and taken rooms. They had all agreed to meet at the saloon in an hour, after they'd all had a chance to wash some of the trail dust off their stinking bodies.

All but Oppie Shenker. Oppie had passed out on the bed the minute he hit the room.

Ramsey and Hutch had come into the hotel lobby just as Fess was leaving for the saloon. Ramsey had told him that the Indians had raided Bolt's ranch, but Ramsey didn't know any more than that. He didn't know if Bolt had been killed, or if Bolt had even been at the ranch. Ramsey said that he'd have one drink with the men before he went to bed, and Hutch had planned on staying at the bar little longer.

But nobody had shown up and Fess was on this third drink already.

"All dressed up and no place to go," the man next to him said.

Fess glanced up at the man's reflection in the mirror and was relieved that the fellow wasn't speaking to him.

He didn't feel like getting into a bullshitting match with strangers tonight.

"The name's Joe. You want whiskey?" asked the tall, emaciated barkeep.

"Yes, please." said the brothers in unison.

"God, I feel sorry for Bolt and the others," said Dale Rader.

Fess Grodin's interest in the men flared at the mention of Bolt. He looked up at the mirror, fixed his gaze on the man right next to him.

"So do I," said his brother.

Fess shifted his gaze to the other man.

"What's wrong with Bolt?" Joe asked when he set the drinks in front of the Raders. He took a grimy bar towel from his shoulder and wiped up the moisture on the countertop in front of them.

"The Indians raided his place tonight," Ralph said. "Right before we got there."

Fess checked the smile that formed at the corners of his mouth. Ramsey was some leader, some schemer.

"Really?" said Joe. He glanced up at the brothers, wiped the towel around in circles. "I hadn't heard."

"Just happened a little while ago."

"How bad was it?

"Nobody killed," said Dale. "Not yet, anyway."

Fess didn't like the sound of it. What did he mean, not yet?

"Then Bolt didn't get hurt?" Joe asked, still polishing the bartop as he looked at the Rader brother.

Fess shifted his gaze in the mirror again, waited, held his breath.

"No. Bolt wasn't even there when it happened," said Dale. "He came in while we were there."

Damn, thought Fess. Bolt was still alive and Ramsey didn't even know it.

"Yeah, we just talked to Bolt a little while ago," said

Ralph.

"Anybody else get hurt?" the barkeep asked.

"No," said Dale, "but the Indians ran off with two of Bolt's harlots."

Fess Grodin fought the urge to turn and stare at the man beside him. That wasn't in Ramsey's plans. The Indians were supposed to raid the whorehouse and kill Bolt, not steal his damned women. Ramsey's sister. Fess wondered if Linda had been one of the harlots stolen by the Indians. If so, it would be ironic, but he was sure Ramsey wouldn't see it that way.

"Ah, that's a damned shame," said Joe.

Why in the hell didn't the dumb barkeep ask which harlot? Fess wondered.

"Yeah," sighed Dale. "The other harlots are really upset about it."

Which harlots? Grodin's mind screamed.

"I can imagine," said Joe. "Any chance of getting the girls back from the Indians?"

"Yes, we hope so," said Ralph. "Bolt and Tom were heading out to track them just as we left."

"Damn, I hope they catch 'em before the girls are harmed and I hope Bolt strings the Indians up by their balls." Joe made a final swipe to the bar. "Damned Indians. They ought to stick to their own kind." He turned and walked to the other end of the bar where some fellow was banging his glass for service.

Fess couldn't stand the suspense.

"Pardon me," he said politely as he turned to the man on his right. "I heard you talking about Bolt. Do you know which harlots the injuns stole?"

Ralph started to say something, hesitated.

Fess read the suspicion in the man's eyes. "I go out there to Bolt's bordello a lot, so I know all of the gals," he lied. "Linda's my favorite," he said, hoping to bait the man. "I just wondered if she got kidnapped."

Again Ralph opened his mouth and paused. "Bolt didn't say."

Fess knew damned well the fellow was lying, but he didn't dare push it any further. He finished his drink, pushed away from the bar. "Well, I sure hope Bolt gets the gals back safely."

Fess went from the saloon, straight to the hotel. He checked with the room clerk, found out Ramsey's room number. He dashed up the stairs, knocked on Ramsey's door. He put his ear to the door, didn't hear any noise inside the room. He pounded again.

"Ramsey! You in there?"

"Yeah, who is it?" came the sleepy reply.

"It's Fess. I gotta talk to you."

"Just a minute."

Fess heard the heavy footsteps coming across the room. Ramsey opened the door in his shorts and shirt.

"C'mon in, Fess. What is it?"

"Bolt's still alive."

"Are you sure?"

"I just heard it in the saloon from a couple of fells who were just out there and talked to Bolt."

"Damn," Ramsey said. "I was hoping that the Indians had carried him away. Hutch thought he saw an extra rider on one of the horses, but it was too dark to tell."

"Ramsey," Fess said cautiously. "That was a whore that Hutch saw." Fess saw the color drain from Ramsey's face.

"Are you positive?"

"Yeah. The fellows in the bar said that the injuns stole two of the harlots and Bolt was leaving to track 'em down."

"Son of a bitch! Did you find out which harlots?"

"No. The fellow said he didn't know. I hope it isn't Linda."

"Damn, it better not be." Ramsey scratched his chin for a minute. "Go round up the men. We're gonna have to join the chase."

"Tonight?"

"Yes, dammit. Tonight. I sure as hell am not going to let Linda get hurt if the Indians have her."

"Where in hell are the men? They're not in the saloon. I just came from there."

"Some of 'em should still be drinkin'."

"Where? I was at the saloon for more than an hour and nobody showed up."

"We went to the bar here in the hotel," Hutch said. "You must have gone to the wrong saloon."

"Maybe I went to the right saloon, after all," Fess said proudly.

"Maybe you did, at that."

Chapter Fifteen

When Bolt saw the first light of morning, he reined his horse to a halt. It was a good place to stop because they were in a low spot, with rolling hills on both sides and a good view of the flat, open country on the other sides.

It'd been a long, hard night for the three of them. For a good part of the time, the moonlight had made it easy for them to follow the tracks of the Indian ponies, but once the brightness faded away, so did their speed. Twice during the early morning blackness, they'd lost the tracks completely and then lost precious time when they had to backtrack to pick them up again.

"Time to stretch our legs." Every bone in his body ached when he eased himself out of the saddle. He stretched, flexed stiff muscles, walked back to Mary's horse.

"How're you doing?" he asked.

She nodded as she always did when he asked. She hadn't spoken a word since they'd left the ranch the night before and Bolt wondered how long she could keep it up.

She eased down from her horse, stretched, looked like she'd had a full night's sleep.

Bolt studied the pony tracks, then made his way up

one of the slopes to look around, his eyes constantly scanning the ground in search of a shallow grave. When he neared the top, he hugged the ground, eased himself up over the crest. He'd done it a dozen times.

His heart skipped a beat when he looked down into the next valley and saw the small band of sleeping Indians. It was still shadowy dark down there, but he spotted Linda and Cathy right away. Their bright gowns set them apart from the Indians.

The only Indian who was awake glanced up the slope and seemed to look right at Bolt. Bolt wanted to duck behind cover, but remained perfectly still. The Indian's gaze was only a passing glance and did not linger on Bolt. The Indian turned away and looked up the opposite slope.

Bolt wanted to scream for joy. Instead he scrambled down the easy slope, careful not to make a sound. Tom looked over at him, started to say something. Bolt put a finger to his lips, pointed up to the top of the slope.

Tom understood the message and smiled. Mary understood his gestures, too. She opened her mouth to say something, caught herself just in time.

"They're over there," Bolt whispered when they had clustered together. "The girls. Seven Indians. Sleeping. All but one."

"Can we get them?" Tom whispered. He made the gesture of going up the hill.

"No. Too risky for girls. We sneak up from behind." He motioned for Tom and Mary to follow him on foot.

They went back the way they had come into the gully, snuck around the end. Bolt stuck his head around the last bit of covering and pointed toward the spot.

There was no one there. No one in sight as far as he could see.

"Damn it," he whispered. "They were all sleeping

there just a few minutes ago. Where'd they go?"

Tom looked and shrugged his shoulders.

"Well, we know we're closing in on them," Bolt said when they got back to their horses. "And the girls are still alive. We'll get them."

It went that way all day. The land became more rugged, with ravines crisscrossing everywhere. Three or four times they spotted the group of Indian riders on a distant hill or in a ravine, but by the time they could get anywhere close, the Indians had disappeared.

In the middle of the afternoon, Bolt spotted a small town ahead. He wasn't surprised. There had been more and more cabins as they rode along. He'd noticed something else as the day wore on. A couple of times he'd noticed a small group of riders behind them, but he hadn't paid much attention to them. But now they were beginning to bother him.

"I think we're being followed," he told Tom.

Tom glanced over his shoulder. "Yeah, I've seen 'em, too."

"Keep your eyes open, front and back," Bolt cautioned.

The trio passed the small town late in the afternoon, when the sun was sinking into the earth. They hadn't seen the Indians for several hours. They pushed on, followed the Indian tracks up and down the hills, knowing that they were being followed.

At dusk, half an hour later, they rode up one hill and Bolt got the shock of his life when he looked down into the valley and saw the Indians. Dozens of them. Braves. Squaws. Maidens, he supposed. And there, in the middle of all of the Indians, were Cathy and Linda in their bright-colored frocks.

Bolt looked through his binoculars and saw the fire ring, the steaming pots. He saw that everyone was eating, including the two girls.

159

"Looks like we got our big chance," Bolt smiled.

"Damn, how are we going to do it?" Tom asked. "They've got us outnumbered ten to one."

"Tom, I'd like you to ride back to that last town and see if you can round up some help. I'll keep my eyes on the Indians."

Tom rode back to town and tried his damndest to get some reinforcements. But he got the same response every time he asked. At the saloon, he approached a giant of a man, rough-looking, mean eyes. He sat down at the fellow's table, told him what he wanted.

"Squaws is squaws. Whores is whores," the ruffian told Tom. "The world won't miss neither one."

Tom was just about ready to give up when he noticed two more hardcases sitting at a back table. He started to approach them, thought better of it. The big fat one, with his back to Tom, was one of the riders who followed them. Tom was sure of it. He turned his head away and listened to their talk.

"Too bad Ramsey had to kill those injun gals we kidnapped," said the one who was drunk.

Ramsey. Linda Ramsey. Did she have a husband who hated Bolt? A brother, or an uncle? Whatever it was, that was the connection he'd been looking for.

"Not so loud," the fat man warned.

"I think it's funny that Gray Wolf turned around and stole Ramsey's sister."

Tom had everything he needed. He plunked a coin on the table and strolled out the door.

With Tom's information, Bolt made his move. The three of them snuck up to the Indian camp on foot, hid out in the bushes that surrounded the round gully.

Bolt waited for more than thirty minutes before he got his chance. When Gray Wolf walked off by himself, away from the clatter of his people, Bolt stalked him. He snuck up behind him, pistol in hand, knew he could kill him with one shot. That wasn't what he wanted.

"Gray Wolf," he whispered.

Gray Wolf swung around, stared at the pistol, then up at Bolt's face.

"The name's Bolt. You got my women and I want them back."

Bolt thought the Indian was going for his tomahawk. Instead, Gray Wolf just stared at him.

"You are not the one who killed my sister," he said.

"No," said Bolt. "Don't take out your revenge on me and my girls. The man you want is named Ramsey. We will help you get him."

"There is bad blood between whites and Comanches," Gray Wolf said firmly.

"What Ramsey did to your chief and to your maidens has made bad blood between him and the whites, too."

"I have seen them follow us. I thought you were a part of them."

"No."

"They have taken on many men since night comes. My scouts tell me this."

"You won't make it unless my partner and I help you," Bolt told him. "All I ask is that you don't touch my girls. If I can show them unharmed, your people will be left alone. I can't ever bring back your sister or the chief's daughter. I can give you only your own life and the lives of your band."

"Yes. I think you are right," Gray Wolf said after careful thought.

"Then tell your people that we will join them."

"Yes, I tell them. You bring your friends here. You stay the night in our camp. We will welcome you."

"We would like that, Gray Wolf."

Gray Wolf started to walk away, but turned to face Bolt again.

"When the sun comes up, I will take you to the buffalo lands," he said with a great deal of pride. "I know of a good place to set up an ambush. That is where I planned to lead you and your men. That is where I planned to kill you in the morning."

Bolt hoped the Comanche didn't see him shudder.

Bolt went back to Tom and Mary, who waited for him in the bushes.

"Well, I wangled us an invitation to supper," he smiled.

"How about a soft bed and a warm woman?" Tom laughed. "Or is it the other way around?"

"Afraid you'll have to wangle that for yourself."

Bolt turned to Mary.

"You can speak now," he grinned.

But Mary Beth Piper only smiled.

Chapter Sixteen

The Indians sat in a wide circle that night and feasted on buffalo stew and corn bread.

As honored guests, Bolt and Tom sat facing Gray Wolf. Mary sat between Bolt and Tom, and Linda and Cathy sat on either side.

Gray Wolf was also flanked by pretty girls—Blue Quail and White Buffalo, two maidens from the tribe that had just joined Gray Wolf that day. Actually, it was the other way around. Gray Wolf had traveled to this place and joined the tribe that was already camped there.

Bolt felt the warmth of the girls who sat beside him and pressed their shoulders against his.

But most of all, he felt the warmth from Blue Quail's soft dark eyes. She flashed them at him all during the meal. It got to be a game between them. Every time Bolt glanced over at Blue Quail and caught her looking at him, she would smile and coyly turn away. Then Bolt would look away. But neither one of them could resist the urge, just to peek, to see if the other was watching.

"Thank you for the feast," Bolt told Gray Wolf when everyone was through eating.

"The feast will come tomorrow night," Gray Wolf

said. He rose from the ground, a signal for the others to rise.

"We must use extra care tonight," he told his people. "The women will all sleep down at that end of the village." He pointed his arm, one finger straight. "In the teepees, where it is safer. I will post guards all around to keep you safe in the night."

"All of us?" Linda asked.

"Yes," Gray Wolf said. "All women will sleep in the teepees. The men will sleep over there." He made a wide, sweeping gesture with his other arm. "We must retire early because tomorrow we have much to do. We must get up before the sun."

Cathy turned to Bolt as the Indians began to chatter.

"We can't tell you how grateful we are for your coming after us," she said.

"I'm glad you're safe," Bolt hugged her.

"We would have all died in the morning," Linda Ramsey said. "I heard them talking, and they were going to rape us and murder us before your eyes. And then they were going to kill you."

"I know," said Bolt. He wrapped his arm around her, drew her close. "But you and Cathy are safe. That's all that matters."

Mary stood nearby, pleased by the way Bolt treated his women.

Bolt stepped over to Gray Wolf.

"Thank you, and sleep well," Bolt said.

"Yes, I think we will all sleep well this night. Even the men who still follow us will sleep."

"I'm sure they will," Bolt said. "After riding all night and day, they must be as tired as we are."

"Do you have any other needs this night?" Gray Wolf asked.

Bolt couldn't help but glance at Blue Quail, who stood next to the chief. Bolt caught her eye just before

164

she smiled and coyly turned away.

"I reckon not," Bolt answered.

Bolt couldn't get to sleep, even though he was bone-assed tired. He sat up on his blanket and looked around.

The men's blankets were scattered out for safety reasons; Bolt slept off to himself behind some bushes, where it was quiet. From there he could see Gray Wolf's blanket and those of many of the men. He could see most of the guards, but he couldn't see the teepees from that angle. But the way he was situated behind the tree, very few of them could see him.

He didn't know why he couldn't sleep. Too tired, he guessed. Or maybe it was because he was thinking about tomorrow. Or was it the look in Blue Quail's eyes that kept him awake? He didn't know. All of the reasons, probably. His flirtations with the pretty little maiden during dinner had been just that — a playful exchange of glances. They meant nothing to him. Nor to her either, he imagined.

He looked at the guards who were posted around and laughed. Even if he wanted to, there was no way he could sneak into her teepee.

He stretched, flexed saddle-sore muscles. Just before he stretched out again, he saw movement near Gray Wolf. He bolted upright, started for his pistol. Then he saw who it was.

Bolt saw Gray Wolf reach up for Linda Ramsey and pull her down onto his blanket. He saw their bodies meld together in an embrace.

Bolt didn't know how long he slept. One moment he was deep in sleep, the next he was wide awake, staring at the stars. No dreams. No warning. The stars had moved, he knew that, and the night seemed close and quiet, the shadows still. Yet, there had been something. Something had awakened him. He listened intently for any sound, any footpad, or rustle of cloth.

A feeling came over him that he was not alone. It was subtle, like a feather tickling the lobe of his ear, the trace of a fingernail along the back of his neck. But it was there, and his senses came to full alert as his eyes adjusted to the darkness.

He listened to the sound of his own breath, felt the beat of his heart in his chest, heard the faint throb of blood at his temple.

Then a shadow moved. Or seemed to move. The movement was very imperceptible, but almost palpable. He tensed, braced himself. His muscles corded up and he started moving his hand toward the pistol under the blanket near his head. He was in an awkward position. If the shadow came closer, if it really was moving, then he would have to dive for his weapon. Better that, than take a knife in the brisket, go down without a fight.

The shadow did move, and this time, he made out a figure on its knees, crawling toward him. Yet, strangely, he felt no menace in the motion. The figure, or creature, was doubled up, impossible to identify.

He slid his hand under the blanket, felt the hardwood of his pistol butt. He snaked it free, pulled on the trigger to muffle the sound of the sear as he cocked the hammer. The mechanism made a little *snick* and he brought the pistol up, ready to aim and fire.

"Bolt," someone whispered, and the shadow moved closer, the person crawling faster.

Still, he held his pistol at the ready.

"Who in hell are you?" he whispered.

"Be still, Bolt. I am Blue Quail."

Relief flooded through him and he eased the hammer back down, gripping the ear with his thumb. He pointed the muzzle downward, toward the ground. He didn't want to shoot Blue Quail by accident—or any other way.

She closed on him, and he saw that she wore only a blanket. She put her mouth to his and he fell back under her soft weight.

"You'll likely get us both killed," he husked, the want in him rising up raw and unbidden, the heat surging through his loins.

The Indian maiden giggled softly, slid a tongue inside his mouth. He reached up for her, felt the softness of her breasts, the nubbins of her nipples, and desire raced through him like a wildfire.

"Blue Quail want to make fuck," she said bluntly, and the words, alien to his white man's ears, were oddly thrilling.

"What if we get caught?" he asked, feeling stupid, unnerved by her bold presence.

"We make little quiet fuck," she said, her voice a faint whisper in his ear. She pressed against him, grinding her loins into his, and he felt his cock arch with engorged blood, push back against the lips of her sexcleft.

"Yes, damned right," he gasped. "Let me get out of my damned clothes first, woman."

She giggled again and the notes of her voice were like a melody in his ears. She tugged at his shirt, fumbled with his buckle. Her bare flesh rubbed against his as he stripped out of his clothes. She rolled beneath him, on her back, and drew him atop her with surprisingly strong arms. He kissed her, found the moistness of her mouth, the tantalizing meat of her tongue. His cock throbbed with the rush of fresh blood and he slid it along the inside of her thigh as he gripped

167

her in strong, sinewy arms.

Blue Quail wriggled beneath, moved her sex against his cock, scooted her hips up and down until his seepage oiled the portal to her cunt. He touched a breast, teased the nipple with a single taunting finger until it hardened like an acorn.

"Bolt, give me fuck," she breathed, her accent strong.

"Yes," he breathed, and took the nipple in his mouth as her hand grasped his cock, squeezed it until he could hear the roar of his own blood in his ears.

She stroked him with a practiced hand, and he realized how sensual she was, how much a woman she was. He had thought her a mere girl, flirting with a white man, but this was a full-blown woman—and she knew how to please a man. Her fingers played him like a violin, moving over his scrotum and up the shaft of his swollen cock, stroking the insides of his thighs. She arched her back, then, drew him to the swollen lips of her pussy. He rose up on stiffened forearms, slid inside her.

She gasped, began to hump against him until he picked up the rhythm, plumbed her warm, moist depths. She was no virgin, and her clasp was strong as she gripped his cock, flexed womanly muscles that squeezed it, shot sparks of pleasure through him.

"Bolt fuck good," she said.

"So does Blue Quail," he replied, and he took her slow, felt her buck with the spasms of joy, felt her flesh ripple with pleasure. He felt her fingers rake his back, but she did not claw him.

"More, give more," she said, struggling with the English words, and he drove into her, drove deep, pushing to the sucking mouth of her womb. He heard her cry out as her body shook beneath him, and then she sobbed as she convulsed again.

His excitement raced now, and he ground his hips

into hers, bore into her with savage thrusts, pumping faster and faster until her orgasms became one long quake of mindless ecstasy and her fingers dug into his back as she held on. She shook her head from side to side and he felt his own juices boil and knew he could not stay the floodtide of his seed any longer.

"Good fuck, good fuck," she said, over and over, and Bolt let himself go. He grasped her back, drew her close to him as he rose to the heights. His body shuddered as he shot his milky seed. She cried out softly, in Comanche, and the word made him shiver with the pleasure of it.

"Good fuck. Blue Quail happy."

"I'm happy too," he said, as the seed drained from him and he felt a lassitude come over him like a warm wave.

He fell atop her, breathing hard from the exertion. Later, he rolled to one side, and she kissed him on the mouth and all over his face. He felt at peace with the night sky, the earth.

He lay there, dozing, and perhaps he slept, for when he awoke again, Blue Quail was gone. He sat up, looked for her, wondered if she would be back.

An owl made a raspy crow and he heard the far-off yap of a coyote. Then it was still, and he thought of Blue Quail and was happy that she had come to him and given him her body under the stars. And his throat ached until he shook off the moment of emptiness that strangled him, until he put the woman out of his mind like a man snuffing out a cigarette after a good smoke.

Chapter Seventeen

Bolt's eyes narrowed to slits. A pair of furrows creased his forehead in twin lines of worry.

"What the hell, Bolt?" asked Tom, tugging on his friend's arm, drawing him away from the Indians. "We in a bad spot?"

"This is a deathtrap, Tom. We lost Ramsey's bunch, but I'd say he has the advantage. Look at this country. Scarred like the back of a flayed sailor, dry as tinder. I don't like it much."

Gray Wolf and Turtle Belly squatted a few yards away, talking fast, gesturing with wide swings of their hands. The other braves stood around them. Bolt could swear they were nervous. That made him nervous.

He looked around again, saw the long ravine that was open at both ends, a shallow draw that could be used as an escape route if they were pressed. They were outnumbered, but if they could draw Ramsey down into this ravine, box him in . . .

"What the hell are they talking about?" Penrod asked, pointing to the Indians.

"Probably the same thing we are, with one difference."

"What's that?"

"They know this place. Look around."

"Brush. Sage. What's so special about it?"

"Look at the buffalo skulls. All facing east. ·Bones everywhere. Dried dung."

"So?" Tom's face wrinkled in puzzlement. He thumbed his left sideburn, squinted as he looked at a bleached ribcage below the bank of the ravine.

"The Comanches hunted here. Killed buffalo, skinned them out. Maybe this is a box."

"Huh?"

"I thought this ravine might be open on two ends. But, likely not. That means we can't go back, and we can't get out on this side. The only way out would be up that narrow draw." He pointed to the place where the wall of the ravine opened to a gully that showed signs of previous flash floods. The entrance was choked with a tangle of mesquite, wormwood, tumbleweeds, sand.

Tom opened his mouth to say something, but was distracted by Gray Wolf and Turtle Belly, who stood up, looked in their direction. Gray Wolf signed for Bolt to come to him. Bolt strode away, leaving Tom to scramble after him.

Before he reached Gray Wolf, the Indian spoke in rapid Comanche to Walking Stick. The old warrior grunted, caught up his pony. He mounted it, rode off in the direction where they last knew Ramsey to be.

"Where's he going?" asked Bolt, when he drew near.

"Scout," said Gray Wolf. "You open your ears. Gray Wolf has words for you."

"I'm listening," said Bolt. Tom crowded near. None of them noticed Linda, who strained to hear every word.

Gray Wolf ordered his braves to make a wide circle. He squatted, beckoning for all the others to do the same. He picked up a dried mesquite stick, drew a crooked line in the dirt.

"This place long, good to kill buffalo. Walking Stick go find Ramsey, bring here." He made marks in the dirt, poked holes to indicate men following the old brave. "They come here." He made a big mark, pointed to a place two hundred yards up the ravine where it made a bend. "He ride fast, get away. Bites Mad Dog, he wait here, make pony walk lame." He pointed to the head of the shallow draw. "Walking Stick help Bites Mad Dog, then ride off, away. Bites Mad Dog waits. We wait. Boy comes in and go away. Ramsey ride in and we shoot bad white men. One and one. Kill all."

Linda gasped inaudibly, her emotions torn to shreds by the talk of killing. She hated Jack Ramsey, but after all, he was her brother, her own flesh and blood kin.

"I get it," said Tom. "That old one brings the bunch in here, then the young un' acts like a decoy. We wait in that draw and get them in the crossfire. Pretty neat."

"It might work, said Bolt, reluctantly. "If Ramsey is dumb enough to go in there. He can see it would have to be single file. We'd have to be far enough back to get most of them up the draw, then pick our targets. So, you'd have to have braves all along there, and they'd have to lie low and quiet."

"Huhnh!" grunted Gray Wolf. "Comanche like the earth. Ramsey no see."

Bolt stood up. The others followed.

He looked up and down the ravine again. The sides were steep. Once Ramsey was inside it, he'd have to fight his way out. So would they. His admiration for the Comanches rose several notches. They were not afraid. But, Ramsey and his men were not buffalo, either. He drew breath from the hot dry air and felt his stomach churn, turn queasy.

"What's the matter, Bolt?" asked Tom. "You not sure

of something?"

"We'd best take our positions," he said, "Gray Wolf, you put us where we can do the most good."

Gray Wolf's mouth widened in a grin. The others grinned too, all except for Crooked Arrow, whose face was dark leather, hard as stone.

Gray Wolf spoke to Bites Mad Dog, who mounted his pony, made it walk lame for all to see. Linda, her mouth puckered up, seemed fidgety, nervous, as if she was holding back a scream. She edged away from the men as they led their mounts past the shallow draw, around a bend and a drop-away slope. Linda, curious, followed at a distance, Red Feather watching her without her knowing it. Gray Wolf ground-tied his pony. Tom and Bolt hobbled their horses, noticed that the Comanches tied their animals up in a staggered formation, as if they had done this many times before. Each man would know where his horse was when the time came.

Satisfied, Gray Wolf led them all back to the draw. He put Red Feather at the opening. When Bolt looked back over his shoulder a few moments later, he could not see the Indian.

"You here," Gray Wolf said to Penrod, pointing to a crevice in the draw where rushing waters had eaten away the bank. He put Crooked Arrow further down, deeper into the draw, and the man sank to his haunches, pulled tumbleweeds around him until he could no longer be seen. He stationed Moccasins Too Big on the opposite bank, on an angle from Crooked Arrow.

Bolt and Turtle Belly lay flat atop the edge of the draw where it narrowed, flanking it. Gray Wolf took a position a few yard from them. He was perhaps a hundred yards into the draw and had a clear view of half of it. Bolt wondered if this would work. With the braves scattered out like this, they seemed even fewer in number, and two of them were not even there.

Suddenly, Bolt stood up.

"Gray Wolf," he called. "Where's Linda?"

"Come. We find her," said the brave.

In their concentration, they had forgotten about Ramsey's sister. Bolt was almost certain she had not come into the draw with them. He and Gray Wolf loped up the draw. Tom started to rise, but Bolt waved him back.

At the head of the draw, they heard hoofbeats.

Moments later, Walking Stick rode up. His pony was sleek with sweat, its mouth flecked slightly with yellow foam.

He made a sign that the white men were coming. Gray Wolf told him in Comanche where to take his horse. The old brave rode slowly up the ravine to the drop-away.

"Linda!" Bolt called.

There was no answer.

"She must be with the horses," said Bolt, his voice cold and flat. She could ruin everything. He didn't want to think about what might be on her mind. But, she had given them the slip and she had had a reason for it.

"We get her," said Gray Wolf, starting toward the place where the horses were tied or hobbled.

When they were halfway there, they heard sounds of a struggle and Walking Stick shouting in Comanche. Bolt and Gray Wolf stood rooted there as Linda appeared, riding Crooked Arrow's pony. Walking Stick had the pony's tail in his grip, was digging in his moccasined heels trying to stop her. She clapped her heels into the pony's flanks, then wheeled it fast. Walking Stick lost his grip, went flying into the ground. She galloped away, hugged the opposite wall of the ravine, staring at Bolt with defiant eyes.

"Don't try to stop me!" she yelled.

"Linda—you could get killed," he protested. "Go back. All hell's going to break loose here."

"I—I can't!" she shouted. "I—I can't just let you shoot Jack down."

"Son of a bitch," muttered Bolt.

At that moment, Bites Mad Dog appeared around the bend of the ravine, his pony limping. Above the ravine, Bolt saw a thin cloud of dust rising against the blue sky. He and Gray Wolf took positions behind a clump of tumbleweeds where they could not be seen.

"They come now," said Gray Wolf. He lifted his rifle, started to bring it down to a point of aim on Linda.

Bolt knocked the barrel of the rifle down.

Anger flared in Gray Wolf's eyes. Walking Stick got to his feet, retreated to get his rifle as Bites Mad Dog rode closer. His pony no longer limped as he urged it into a fast trot.

"No," Bolt said to Gray Wolf, as Linda broke into a gallop. "Let her go. If she tells Ramsey where we are, then that will have to be. We still have the advantage." He drew a breath, deep. "Some," he said lamely.

"White bitch," Gray Wolf muttered.

"The shot would drive them back, anyway, said Bolt, knowing it was now too late to stop Linda, to stop whatever was going to happen. They were caught between a rock and a hard place now. The cloud of dust in the sky grew thicker and Bites Mad Dog rode up on them, panting from lack of breath. Gray Wolf waved him on by, spoke instructions in rapid Comanche. The young brave disappeared around the bend.

Ramsey and four of his men galloped into view, saw Linda riding toward them. Ramsey wheeled his horse, but Linda rode into the center of the ravine, sobbing hysterically.

"Oh, Jack," she shouted, "go back quick. They're going to kill you. They're waiting for you."

Bolt put a hand on Gray Wolf's arm. The Comanche had started to bring his rifle up again. His dark eyes were agates, sunk into deep sockets.

"Let her play it out," Bolt said softly.

If Linda expected her brother to welcome her with open arms, she was sadly mistaken. Ramsey hauled up on his reins. The other four outlaws drew up behind him. Linda stopped the pony, leaped from its back.

"Jack. . . ."

"You slut," he said. "You reek of Comanche stink. You gave your body to Gray Wolf, didn't you?"

"No!" she protested. "Jack, you've got to listen to me. . . ."

Ramsey leaped from his horse, his face contorted with rage. He waded into his sister, swung a chopping hand toward her face. His palm smashed into her cheek and Linda spun away, dazed by the blow.

A muscle in Bolt's jaw rippled the flesh.

Walking Stick and Bites Mad Dog, hugging the bank like two shadows, slinked up behind Bolt and Gray Wolf. The Comanche leader waved them into the mouth of the draw. The two braves disappeared like smoke.

Ramsey flew into an insane rage. As Bolt watched helplessly, the brutal man began to beat her, slamming fists into her face and stomach, yelling obscenities at her.

Linda screamed, and the sound was so chilling Bolt almost ran from cover. He had never wanted to kill a man so much as he wanted now to kill Jack Ramsey.

Ramsey's men spoke together, then dismounted. In a body, they ran toward Ramsey, pulled him, blubbering, off his sister.

"You don't beat no woman like that," said one man.

176

"Especially your goddamned sister."

"That fuckin' whore!" screamed Ramsey.

Linda, terrified, got to her feet, started running toward the draw. Ramsey tried to draw his pistol, but his men restrained him.

"Let her go, Ramsey."

Bolt saw the terror in her face, stepped from behind the clump of tumbleweeds. She ran toward him, her cheeks streaked with tears.

"Oh, Bolt," she wailed, "what have I done?"

Before he could answer, the air crackled with explosions as Ramsey and his men drew pistols, began firing at Linda.

"Get down!" Bolt shouted, going into a crouch. He levered a round into the chamber of his rifle, dropped to one knee.

"It's a trap, boys," said Ramsey, his hysteria wiped out by the smoke of battle. That bitch sister of mine drew us into a trap!"

Linda stumbled and went down as bullets whined overhead, fried the air. Puffs of white smoke dotted the far side of the ravine.

Bolt fired, then retreated under a hail of lead. Ramsey and his men backed toward their horses, remounted, and drew rifles from scabbards.

"Come!" said Gray Wolf, firing at Ramsey to give Bolt cover.

"I've got to get Linda out of here," Bolt said, but he knew it was no use. Bullets kicked up dust spurts all around him. Linda lay still. Perhaps, he thought, she was already dead.

He rolled over on his back, fired another round, then ran a zigzag pattern to the mouth of the draw.

Ramsey barked orders and two of his men galloped off, back down the ravine. They disappeared and Bolt knew that any chance of an ambush was gone. He felt a bullet tug at his sleeve as he dove headlong into the shallow draw. Rifle fire erupted all around him. He lifted himself on one arm, turned to see if any of the bullets had struck Ramsey and the remaining two men. But the trio rode off and the sound of their hoofbeats slowly faded into a long deep silence.

Bolt stood up, stiff and sore.

Gray Wolf appeared a moment later, a dark scowl on his face.

In the distance they heard the white men shouting, and a thunder of hoofbeats.

"Well, Gray Wolf," said Bolt. "You got any more ideas? In about two minutes they'll have this ravine sealed off. We can stay here and eat dirt, or shoot our way out."

"We stay. Maybe they come back, look for us."

"Yeah," said Bolt, "maybe."

The two men stood there, listening, as the sounds of hoofbeats, the shouts of the outlaws, died away.

"Maybe," Bolt said again, softly, to himself.

Then, they heard it.

The sound, like no other. And, as the breeze whipped against their faces, they smelled it.

Fire. And smoke.

Bolt did not look at Gray Wolf, but fought down the quivering fear that boiled in his stomach.

A line of men, like shadow sticks, appeared beyond the crook of the ravine. They tossed burning tumbleweeds onto dry grasses. Black smoke swirled, traced fingers in the sky.

"We're trapped here," said Bolt. "Better get your men. We've got to make a move or cook like Kansas grasshoppers in a prairie fire."

Behind them, above the draw, from another direction, smoke blotted out the sky and the air grew hot as the fire crackled toward the draw.

"Bolt," yelled Penrod, as he came running up. "I don't like this none."

"Welcome to Hades," said Bolt wryly. "A little too early to suit me."

"Jared, this ain't a damned bit funny."

No, Bolt thought.

It wasn't funny at all.

Chapter Eighteen

Gray Wolf made a series of high-pitched yelps. The other braves emerged from their hiding places, gathered around him at the mouth of the draw. The fire at the head of the east end of the ravine was still several hundreds of yards away. The wind whipped it, sent showers of sparks shooting up into the air. Behind and above them, they could hear the distant roar of flames.

"We go," said Gray Wolf.

As if to punctuate his words, they all heard the shrieking whinnies of their horses. Smoke blackened the sky to the east and north, but only wisps of it curled over the edge of the ravine toward the western end.

"Wait a minute," said Bolt, his mind racing. "Maybe we can use this brush fire to advantage."

"What you mean?" asked Gray Wolf.

"Ramsey thinks we're trapped in here. He's got men above us to the north, and men sealing us off from the east. But to the west, it's clear. How far does this ravine go?"

"Far. Much steep. Go down into canyon. Long way."

"No good," said Bolt. "We've got to find a way out, farther down. Any little draws like this one?"

"Hmm. Maybe," said Gray Wolf. He began to speak in Comanche to the other braves. Moccasins Too Big spoke rapidly in reply, made signs in the air with his hands.

"Well?" asked Tom, impatient, his eyes wide as he watched the billowing smoke roll over the ravine. Soon, it would boil down to where they stood, strangling them. They had to move, and fast, if they were going to get out alive.

"Him say many little places where the water runs, cuts open the land. We look, maybe find a place. Why you ask this? We ride to end of ravine, away from fire and choking smoke."

"I'm thinking we can not only get out, but surprise Ramsey and his men. Turn this defeat into a victory," said Bolt quietly. "Will you let me give it a try? If your braves do what I tell them, we just might take those bastards down."

Gray Wolf grinned widely.

"You tell Gray Wolf. Gray Wolf tell braves you leader now."

Tom shifted his weight on his feet for the tenth time, looked at Bolt as if his friend had taken leave of his senses.

"Jared," he said, "you better make it damn quick. I can smell bacon about to fry and I sure as hell don't want it to be mine."

Bolt drew a breath, knew there was not much time. Before he could speak, he heard a scream. Turning he saw Linda rise from the ground, a tongue of flame racing toward her like the lava flow from a volcano.

Ramsey laughed fiendishly as he saw the flames build a wall of fire across the gateway to the ravine.

"They won't get out of there alive," he slobbered, his lips slick with spittle. The fire excited him. The thought of killing Bolt and the Comanches made his face flush with racing blood.

"They come of there, boys," he said, "we shoot them down like fish in a barrel."

"They sure as hell can't climb out of there on horseback," said Shenker. "And if they ride through that fire, we can sure as hell pick 'em off."

The fire atop the plateau raged out of control, whipped by the wind. Smoke boiled out of the blazing grass, sending waves of heat in their direction.

"If it ever gets up that draw," said Ramsey, "they'll be cooked for sure." He cackled at the thought.

"What if they wait it out?" asked Kyle Hutchinson. "Do we ride in there after them?"

"Hell, Hutch," said Ramsey, "that ravine is like a damned chimney. Wind barrels down through there, they'll have to move. You all get ready. We're going to shoot us some Comanch' and I'll have Bolt's hide tacked to the barn door before nightfall."

As if in reply, the flames surged through the entrance to the ravine, swept toward the draw as if sucked there by an invisible force. Ramsey checked the rounds in his rifle, licked his lips in anticipation of the kill.

"Linda!" Bolt shouted. He raced toward her, grabbed her as she stumbled. He folded her into his arms. "Come on," he said to her, "we're going to get out of here."

The two of them staggered back toward Tom Penrod and the Comanches. Linda choked on smoke, but held up. She didn't seem to be hurt badly.

"Come on," said Bolt. "To the horses. I'll tell you my plan on the way."

The bunch moved quickly up the ravine. Behind them, a giant finger of flame jumped the plateau and dove into the draw. Fire swept through it like through a chimney flue and Tom shuddered as he ran after Bolt on ungainly legs.

"We stay here, we'll be cooked," said Bolt, holding onto Linda so that she would not fall. "If we try and make it out the way we came in, we'll catch lead for sure."

"You speak straight," said Gray Wolf.

They came upon their mounts. Some of the ponies had bolted and dragged their horsehair reins. Bolt's horse whickered with fear as he cut the hobbles. Tom had trouble getting the hobbles off his horse, and his curses turned the dry air blue. Linda grabbed up her pony as Crooked Arrow chased after his, finally cornering it against the far side of the widening ravine.

They rode in a bunch down the west slope of the ravine, saw it deepen. Then, Bolt saw the cuts where floodwaters had gobbled the soft earth.

"I'm going to split us into two groups," Bolt told Gray Wolf. "You take half your braves up one of those arroyos, I'll take Tom and the others up one on the opposite side."

"Why you do this?" asked the Comanche leader.

"I'll catch Ramsey on his left flank, you'll ride wide and catch him on the right flank. It'll be like pinching him in with two fingers." Bolt made the sign. "We can use the smoke for cover. He won't be expecting us from either direction."

"You would make a good Comanche," said Gray Wolf, grinning.

"All I want to be now, is a live white man," said Bolt, choking on smoke. "Now let's get moving."

Gray Wolf ordered Bites Mad Dog, Walking Stick, and Crooked Arrow to go with him up the narrow arroyo to the north. He told the others to go with Bolt. None protested his decision. The fire hurtled toward them, blotting out the east end of the ravine. From the north, the blaze held steady, blocked by the draw where they had been. There, the fire raged in full fury.

Bolt found another arroyo, this one much steeper than the one Gray Wolf had used, but passable. He and Moccasins Too Big led the way, with Red Feather and Tom following after Linda. There were not many of them, Bolt knew, but if they could circle the ravine, come up on Ramsey's left flank, they had a chance to even the numbers up some.

The riders scrambled to the top of the arroyo. Chunks of earth broke loose, spooked the horses. On the high plateau, they looked down, saw the sea of flames racing down the ravine. In seconds, it reached the place where they had been, now funneled up the arroyos like something sentient, something horrible.

Bolt shuddered, flicked his arm toward the east, clapped spurs to his horse's flanks. They rode through smoke, hunched over their mounts, blinked eyes that burned with the acrid fumes. Tears welled in Bolt's eyes and for a long time he wondered if he had made the right decision. They rode into uncertain danger, drawing closer to their objective, and the smoke got thicker. But at least, he thought, the fire was contained in the ravine. The horses galloped, wide-eyed with fear, along the edge of the sheer drop-off, Bolt in the lead.

Then he saw them, Ramsey's men on horseback, well back of the flames. They had rifles across their pommels.

"There," he said, reining up. "Scatter and go into them. Pick your targets, Tom." He signed to the Comanches, then put a finger to his lips. He didn't want them riding down there yelling out their lungs. He looked across the flaming ravine, but saw only clouds of thick smoke. No sign of Gray Wolf and his men.

"After we take out this bunch, then home in on me. We have to play the rest of it Comanche style. He signed as best he knew how until the Indians nodded that they understood him.

"Now!" he yelled, spurring his horse forward as he drew his rifle up above his waist. He thumbed back the hammer, picked out a man on his left, and arrowed toward him.

Bolt fired, cut down his first man. Rifle fire erupted all around him and he saw other men fall.

Scattered shots told him the positions of Ramsey's men. He saw their surprised faces as he shot them out of their saddles. No sign of Ramsey himself, and Bolt figured he was atop the other side of the plateau, waiting to fire on them if they came up from the west.

The Comanches rode up on unsuspecting men, shot them from their mounts. Tom worked the edge of the ravine, shot two men who tried to run away, shouting a warning to Ramsey.

The firing dwindled, died away. Bolt made a sign, drawing the other to his side. He looked around, but saw no sign of Linda.

"Get off your horses," he ordered.

"Damn, Jared, we ought to go on. We've got the bastards on the run."

"No." He made sign to the braves. He got off his horse, hugged the ground; the Comanches did the same. Tom didn't hurry, but kept looking through the smoke, hesitating. "Goddammit, Tom, get down. So far, Ramsey doesn't know we took out his left flank. He'll puzzle over it awhile, then come a-lookin'. We'll be ready."

"How can you be so damned cock-sure?" Tom asked sarcastically.

"Because Ramsey smells blood, and . . . listen."

They all heard it. The thunder of horses' hooves on hard ground. Tom jumped off his horse, hit the ground flat.

They waited, as the ponies and horses milled. The sound of hoofbeats drew closer. So far, Bolt thought, Gray Wolf and his braves hadn't fired a shot. But there was more smoke on that side, and they had a wider circle to make. If his hunch was right, this would work to his advantage.

"Ram, I think them Comanch's and Bolt have broke through down there, said Hutch. "Hear them shots?"

"Sounds like our boys, all right," said Big Mac Sloan.

"Listen," said Ramsey, not yet sure.

The rifle fire faded and then grew strong for several moments.

"About the onliest way they could get out," said Zeke Wiley, who slumped in his saddle, fingering the trigger guard on his rifle.

Ramsey, wary as a coyote, did not say anything for a long time. Instead, he listened to the rifle fire, mulled it over in his mind. The firing became more sporadic, finally died away.

"What do you think, Ram?" asked Vern.

"Awful quiet," said Hutch. "Reckon it's all over?"

"Shit," said Ramsey. "Let's go see. I figure my boys had the advantage. Those were all good men."

But his voice quavered and his men knew he was not sure. And if he wasn't sure, neither were they. They galloped to the south, following Ramsey, their guns at the ready.

A few moments later, Ramsey saw the Indian ponies. His face lit up. He failed to see the horses of his men. These had run off after losing their riders, and were far away from the smoke and fire.

"Looks like they got 'em," said Ramsey. "Those are Injun ponies, and there's Bolt's horse."

"Looky there," said Wiley, pointing. "Ain't that one of your riders, Ram?"

The stillness that followed Wiley's discovery threw a pall over the outlaws.

"Hell, maybe they got one before . . ."

But Ramsey's voice trailed off as his uncertainty rose. He rode on, the others following, but he felt as if he was riding through a graveyard.

Bolt gave the signal, brought his rifle up to his shoulder.

He took aim on Vernon Tate, squeezed the trigger.

The Comanches started firing. Tom's rifle barked and Oppie Shenker clutched at his throat. His hand came away with blood on it as he crumpled, his spine shattered. Ramsey and his men scattered, but to his rear, more rifle fire erupted.

Bolt wanted to shout his exultation. There, beyond the silhouettes of Ramsey and his men, Comanche ponies pounded toward them out of the smoke, and the rifles belched orange flame.

Tom and Bolt boiled up from the ground, began firing on bended knees. The Comanches picked targets, sent deadly lead flying after Ramsey's men. Gray

Wolf and his men made a circle, closed in, blocking off all escape.

Ramsey, in a cowardly move, ran down Hutch in his eagerness to save his own hide. Tom shot Hutch out of the saddle as Bolt caught up his horse, chased after Ramsey.

Ramsey turned, fired his rifle from the hip.

The bullet sizzled past Bolt's ear. He kept coming, his rifle silent. He sheathed it, drew close. Ramsey tried to cock his rifle, lost his grip. The weapon tumbled from his hands. He hauled in on the reins.

"You son of a bitch," he spat. "You fuckin' pimp. You and the goddamned whores. They're all whores, and you made my stupid sister one."

Linda rode up, then, her face blackened by smoke, her hair disheveled.

"Kill him, Bolt," she screamed.

Ramsey drew his pistol then, swung it toward Linda.

"You're evil," he snarled. "You lived like a whore, you'll die like a whore."

Bolt clawed for his pistol, cocked it on the rise. He squeezed the trigger before Ramsey could fire. The outlaw grabbed a spot high on his chest, slid from his saddle, his eyes glazing over with a grayish film.

The Comanches began yelling, killing the last of Ramsey's gang. Bolt dismounted as Linda slid from the pony, ran to her dying brother.

"You slut," Ramsey gasped as Bolt strode up. He saw Bolt, tried to smile. "Ever wonder why I hate women?"

"No. I figured you had a sickness, something wrong inside your head." Linda turned away, began to weep. She slumped to the ground, exhausted.

"My own father married a whore. He kept telling everybody how she had changed, become a good wife.

She gave birth to me and Linda and we had no choice in the matter."

Ramsey choked and something rattled in his throat. Bolt looked at the man's glassy eyes, saw the death coming on like a fog in morning.

"I couldn't get it out of my mind that my own mother had been a whore. I knew Linda would wind up the same way," said Ramsey.

Tom and Gray Wolf came up then, curious.

"No," said Bolt to Ramsey. "Your mother wasn't a whore. She had changed her life. Your father told you that. You should have believed him. You should have changed your life like your mother did. If anyone is responsible for Linda's choice, it wasn't your mother, Ramsey. It was you."

Ramsey looked at Bolt in horror as the words seeped through to his dying brain. He looked then at Linda. She stared back at him with tear-filled eyes. He saw the bruises on her face, reached out and touched one tenderly.

"I'm sorry," he breathed.

The rattle in his throat surged up, shut off his air. He opened his mouth, but no sound came out. His eyes went wide, then frosted over before they closed — forever.

"I—I never knew," Linda said numbly. "Jack never told me about our mother."

"Even if he had," said Bolt, "he would have told you wrong."

"Yes, I see that. Poor Jack."

Gray Wolf touched Bolt's shoulder. Bolt looked up. The Comanche tossed his head, walked away. Bolt stood up, followed him.

"You have much wisdom for a white man," said the Indian, drawing his knife. He cut a gash in his forearm. Bolt watched as blood gushed from the wound.

"Will you be my blood brother, white man?"

Bolt holstered his pistol, rolled up his sleeve, offered his arm. Gray Wolf made the slice, put his arm against Bolt's. Their blood mingled.

Tom looked over in fascination. He knew he had seen something very unusual, something very powerful between men.

Linda and Cathy waited while Bolt finished cinching up his saddle. He patted his bedroll, then put a foot in the stirrup, swung up into the saddle.

Tom, like the girls, already mounted, looked over at Jared.

"I didn't quite savvy all that business with Ramsey and his mother, about how Linda became a whore," he said.

"Ramsey couldn't live with it, Tom. He saw his mother as a whore when she wasn't. He saw his sister as a whore too."

"Well, ain't that what she is?"

"Maybe not, Tom. Maybe Ramsey got what he really wanted. Trouble was, he didn't know what he wanted."

"That don't make no sense, Jared."

Bolt shrugged.

"Let's put it this way, Tom. A little learning can be a dangerous thing. Jack Ramsey listened only to the bad part, something that had already happened and couldn't be changed. He couldn't change it, anyway. He didn't look for the good part."

"What was that?"

"Whatever it was, he never saw it."

"So, is Linda a whore, or ain't she?"

Linda drew a large tortoise-shell comb through her long hair. The sun struck it. She looked beautiful as Bolt winked at her.

"I don't know, Tom," said Jared. "Why don't you ask her sometime?"

Thank you for shopping
at the Book Rack. Please
come again.

WHITE SQUAW
Zebra's Adult Western Series
by E.J. Hunter

#1: SIOUX WILDFIRE   (1205, $2.50)

#2: BOOMTOWN BUST   (1286, $2.50)

#3: VIRGIN TERRITORY   (1314, $2.50)

#4: HOT TEXAS TAIL   (1359, $2.50)

#5: BUCKSKIN BOMBSHELL   (1410, $2.50)

#6: DAKOTA SQUEEZE   (1479, $2.50)

#7: ABILENE TIGHT SPOT   (1562, $2.50)

#8: HORN OF PLENTY   (1649, $2.50)

#9: TWIN PEAKS — OR BUST   (1746, $2.50)

#10: SOLID AS A ROCK   (1831, $2.50)

Available wherever paperbacks are sold, or order direct from the Publisher. Send cover price plus 50¢ per copy for mailing and handling to Zebra Books, Dept. 1866, 475 Park Avenue South, New York, N.Y. 10016. DO NOT SEND CASH.